THE
CRAZY
KILL

CHESTER HIMES

THE
CRAZY
KILL

VINTAGE CRIME / BLACK LIZARD

VINTAGE BOOKS A DIVISION OF RANDOM HOUSE, INC. NEW YORK

All rights reserved under International and Pan-American Copyright
Conventions. Published in the United States by Vintage Books, a
division of Random House, Inc., New York. Originally published
by The Chatham Bookseller, New Jersey, in 1973.

Library of Congress Cataloging-in-Publication Data
Himes, Chester B., 1909–
The crazy kill / Chester Himes.
p.   cm.—(Vintage crime)
"Originally published by the Chatham Bookseller, New Jersey, in
1973"—T.p. verso.

ISBN-13: 978-0-679-72572-5

ISBN-10: 0-679-72572-5

I. Title.
PS3515.I713C7   1989   89-22624
813'.54—dc20   CIP

146028962

1

IT WAS FOUR o'clock, Wednesday morning, July 14th, in Harlem, U.S.A. Seventh Avenue was as dark and lonely as haunted graves.

A colored man was stealing a bag of money.

It was a small white canvas bag, the top tied with a cord. It lay on the front seat of a Plymouth sedan that was double-parked on Seventh Avenue, in front of an A&P grocery store in the middle of the block between 131st and 132nd Streets.

The Plymouth belonged to the manager of the A&P store. The bag contained silver money to be used for making change. The curb was lined with big shiny cars, and the manager had double-parked until he'd unlocked the store and put the money in the safe. The manager didn't want to risk walking a block down a Harlem street at that time of morning with a bag of money in his hand.

There was always a colored patrolman on duty in front of the store when the manager arrived. The patrolman stood guard over the cartons and crates of canned goods, groceries and vegetables, which the A&P delivery truck unloaded on the sidewalk, until the manager arrived.

But the manager was a white man. He didn't trust the streets of Harlem, even with a cop on guard.

The manager's distrust was being justified.

As he stood in front of the door, taking the key from his pocket, with the colored cop standing by his side, the thief sneaked along the other side of the parked cars, stuck his long bare black arm through the open window of the Plymouth and noiselessly lifted the bag of silver money.

The manager looked casually over his shoulder at just the instant the stooping figure of the thief, creeping

5

along the street, was disappearing behind another parked car.

"Stop, thief!" he shouted, assuming the man was a thief on general principles.

Before the words had got clear of his mouth the thief was high-balling for all he was worth. He was wearing a ragged dark green cotton T-shirt, faded blue jeans and dirt-blackened canvas sneakers, which, along with his color, blended with the black asphalt, making him hard to distinguish.

"Where's he at?" the cop asked.

"There he goes!" a voice said from above.

Both the cop and the manager heard the voice, but neither looked up. They had seen a dark blur turning on a sharp curve into 132nd Street, and both had taken off in pursuit simultaneously.

The voice had come from a man standing in a lighted third-story window, the only lighted window in the block of five- and six-story buildings.

From behind the man's silhouetted figure came the faint sounds of a jam session holding forth in the unseen rooms. The hot licks on a tenor sax kept time with the feet pounding on the sidewalk pavement, and the bass notes from a big piano were echoing the light dry thunder of a kettledrum.

The silhouette shortened as the man leaned farther and farther out the window to watch the chase. What had first appeared to be a tall thin man slowly became a short squat midget. And still the man leaned farther out. When the cop and the store manager turned the corner, the man was leaning so far out his silhouette was less than two feet high. He was leaning out of the window from his waist up.

Slowly his hips leaned out. His buttocks rose into the light like a slow-rolling wave, then dropped below the window ledge as his legs and feet slowly rose into the air. For a long moment the silhouette of two feet sitting upside down on top of two legs was suspended in the yellow lighted rectangle. Then it sank slowly from view, like a body going head-down into water.

6

The man fell in slow motion, leaning all the way, so that he turned slowly in the air.

He fell past the window underneath, which bore the black-lettered message:

SMALL CAPS

STRAIGHTEN UP AND FLY RIGHT
Anoint the Love Apples
With Father Cupid's Original
ADAM OINTMENT
A Cure For All Love Troubles

To one side of the cartons and crates was a long wicker basket of fresh bread. The large soft spongy loaves, wrapped in wax paper, were stacked side by side like cotton pads.

The man landed at full length on his back exactly on top of the mattress of soft bread. Loaves flew up about him like the splash of freshly packaged waves as his body sank into the warm bed of bread.

Nothing moved. Not even the tepid morning air.

Above, the lighted window was empty. The street was deserted. The thief and his pursuers had disappeared into the Harlem night.

Time passed.

Slowly the surface of the bread began to stir. A loaf rose and dropped over the side of the basket to the sidewalk as though the bread had begun to boil. Another squashed loaf followed.

Slowly, the man began erupting from the basket like a zombie rising from the grave. His head and shoulders came up first. He gripped the edges of the basket, and his torso straightened. He put a leg over the side and felt for the sidewalk with his foot. The sidewalk was still there. He put a little weight on his foot to test the sidewalk. The sidewalk was steady.

He put his other foot over the edge to the sidewalk and stood up.

The first thing he did was to adjust his gold-rimmed spectacles on his nose. Next he felt his pants pockets to see if he'd lost anything. Everything seemed to be there

7

—keys, Bible, knife, handkerchief, wallet and the bottle of herb medicine he took for nervous indigestion.

Then he brushed his clothes vigorously, as though loaves of bread might be sticking to him. After that he took a big swig of his nerve medicine. It tasted bitter-sweet and strongly alcoholic. He wiped his lips with the back of his hand.

Finally he looked up. The lighted window was still there, but somehow it looked strangely like the pearly gates.

2

DEEP SOUTH WAS shouting in a hoarse bass voice: *"Steal away, daddy-o, steal away to Jesus . . ."*

His meaty black fingers were skipping the light fantastic on the keys of the big grand piano.

Susie Q. was beating out the rhythm on his kettle drum.

Pigmeat was jamming on his tenor sax.

The big luxurious sitting room of the Seventh Avenue apartment was jam-packed with friends and relatives of Big Joe Pullen, mourning his passing.

His black-clad widow, Mamie Pullen, was supervising the serving of refreshments.

Dulcy, the present wife of Big Joe's godson, Johnny Perry, was wandering about, being strictly ornamental, while Alamena, Johnny's former wife, was trying to be helpful.

Doll Baby, a chorus chick who was carrying a torch for Dulcy's brother, Val, was there to see and be seen.

Chink Charlie Dawson, who was carrying a torch for Dulcy herself, shouldn't have been there at all.

The others were grieving out of the kindness of their hearts and the alcohol in their blood, and because grieving was easy in the stifling heat.

Holy Roller church sisters were crying and wailing and

8

daubing at their red-rimmed eyes with black-bordered handkerchiefs.

Dining car waiters were extolling the virtues of their former chef.

Whorehouse madams were exchanging reminiscences about their former client.

Gambler friends were laying odds that he'd make heaven on his first try.

Ice cubes tinkled in eight-ounce glasses of bourbon whisky and ginger ale, black rum and Coca Cola, clear gin and tonic water. Everybody was drinking and eating. The food and liquor were free.

The blue-gray air was thick as split-pea soup with tobacco smoke, pungent with the scent of cheap perfume and hothouse lilies, the stink of sweating bodies, the fumes of alcohol, hot fried food and bad breath.

The big bronze-painted coffin lay on a rack against the wall between the piano and the console radio-television-record set. Flowers were banked about a horse-shoe wreath of lilies as though about a horse in the winner's circle at the Kentucky Derby.

Mamie Pullen said to Johnny Perry's young wife, "Dulcy, I want to talk to you."

Her usually placid brown face, framed by straightened gray hair pulled into a tight knot atop her head, was heavily seamed with grief and fear.

Dulcy looked resentful. "For Chrissake, Aunt Mamie, can't you let me alone?"

Mamie's tall, thin, work-hardened old body, clad in a black satin Mother Hubbard gown that dragged the floor, stiffened with resolve. She looked as though she had been washed with all waters and had come out still clean.

On sudden impulse, she took Dulcy by the arm, steered her into the bathroom and closed and locked the door.

Doll Baby had been watching them intently from across the room. She moved away from Chink Charlie and pulled Alamena to one side.

"Did you see that?"

"See what?" Alamena asked.

"Mamie took Dulcy into the crapper and locked the door."

9

Alamena studied her with sudden curiosity.

"What about it?"

"What they go so secretive to talk about?"

"How the hell would I know?"

Doll Baby frowned. It relieved the set stupidity of her expression. She was a brownskin model type, slim, tan and cute. She wore a tight-fitting flaming orange silk dress and was adorned with enough heavy costume jewelry to sink her rapidly to the bottom of the sea. She worked in the chorus line at Small's Paradise Inn, and she looked strictly on the make.

"It looks mighty funny at a time like this," she persisted, then asked slyly, "Will Johnny inherit anything?"

Alamena raised her eyebrows. She wondered if Doll Baby was shooting at Johnny Perry. "Why don't you ask him, sugar?"

"I don't have to. I can find out from Val."

Alamena smiled evilly. "Be careful, girl. Dulcy's damn particular 'bout her brother's women."

"That bitch! She'd better mind her own business. She's so hot after Chink it's a scandal."

"It's likely to be more than that now Big Joe is dead," Alamena said seriously. A shadow passed over her face.

Once she had been the same type as Doll Baby, but ten years had made a difference. She still cut a figure in the deep purple turtle-neck silk jersey dress she was wearing, but her eyes were the eyes of a woman who didn't care any more.

"Val ain't big enough to handle Johnny, and Chink keeps pressing Dulcy as if he ain't going to be satisfied until he gets himself killed."

"That's what I can't see," Doll Baby said in a puzzled tone of voice. "What's he giving such a big performance for? Unless he's just trying to get Johnny's goat?"

Alamena sighed, involuntarily fingering the collar covering her throat.

"Somebody better tell him that Johnny's got a silver plate in his head and it's sitting too heavy on his brain."

"Who can tell that yellow nigger anything?" Doll Baby said. "Look at him now."

They turned and watched the big yellow man push his

10

way through the crowded room to the door as though enraged about something, then go out and slam the door behind him.

"He's gotta make out like he's mad just because Dulcy went into the crapper to talk to Mamie, when all he's really tryin' to do is get the hell away from her before Johnny comes."

"Why don't you go too and take his temperature, sugar," Alamena said maliciously. "You been holding his hand all evening."

"I ain't interested in that whisky jockey," Doll Baby said.

Chink worked as a bartender in the University Club downtown on East 48th Street. He made good money, ran with the Harlem dandies and could have girls like Doll Baby by the dozen.

"Since when ain't you interested?" Alamena asked sarcastically. "Since he just went out the door?"

"Anyway, I gotta go find Val," Doll Baby said defensively, moving off. She left immediately afterward.

Sitting on the lid of the toilet seat inside of the locked bathroom, Mamie Pullen was saying, "Dulcy, honey, I wish you'd keep away from Chink Charlie. You're making me awfully nervous, child."

Dulcy grimaced at her own reflection in the mirror. She was standing with her thighs pressed against the edge of the washbowl, causing the rose-colored skin-tight dress to crease inside the valley of her round, seductive buttocks.

"I'm trying to, Aunt Mamie," she said, nervously patting her short-cut orange-yellow curls framing the olive-brown complexion of her heart-shaped face. "But you know how Chink is. He keeps putting himself in my face no matter how hard I try to show him I ain't interested."

Mamie grunted skeptically. She didn't approve of the latest Harlem fad of brownskin blondes. Her worried old eyes surveyed Dulcy's flamboyant decor—the rainbow-hued whore-shoes with the four-inch lucite heels; the choker of cultured pink pearls; the diamond-studded watch; the emerald bracelet; the heavy gold charm bracelet; the two diamond rings on her left hand and the ruby ring on

11

her right; the pink pearl earrings shaped like globules of petrified caviar.

Finally she commented, "All I can say is, honey, you ain't dressed for the part."

Dulcy turned angrily, but her hot long-lashed eyes dropped quickly from Mamie's critical stare to Mamie's man-fashioned straight-last shoes protruding from beneath the skirt of Mamie's long black satin dress.

"What's the matter with the way I dress?" she argued belligerently.

"It ain't designed to hide you," Mamie said drily, then, before Dulcy could frame a comment, she asked quickly, "What really happened between Johnny and Chink at Dickie Wells's last Saturday night?"

Dulcy's upper lip began to sweat.

"Just the same old thing. Johnny's so jealous of me sometimes I think he's crazy."

"Why do you egg him on then? Do you just have to switch your ass at every man that passes by?"

Dulcy looked indignant.

"Me and Chink was friends before I even knew Johnny, and I don't see why I can't say hello to him if I want to. Johnny don't take no trouble to ignore his old flames, and Chink never was even that."

"Child, you're not trying to tell all that rumpus come just from you saying hello to Chink."

"You don't have to believe it unless you want to. Me and Val and Johnny was sitting at a ringside table when Chink came by and said, 'Hello, honey, how's the vein holding out?' I laughed. Everybody in Harlem knows that Chink calls Johnny my gold vein, and if Johnny had any sense he'd just laugh, too. But instead of that he jumped up before anybody knew what was happening and pulled his frog-sticker and began shouting about how he was going to teach the mother-raper some respect. So naturally Chink drew his own knife. If it hadn't been for Val and Joe Turner and Big Caesar keeping them apart Johnny would have started chivving on him right there. Didn't nothing really happen though 'cepting they knocked over some tables and chairs. What made it seem like such a big rumpus was some of those hysterical chicks began

12

screaming and carrying on, trying to impress their niggers that they was scared of a little cutting."

She giggled suddenly. Mamie gave a start.

"It ain't nothing to laugh about," Mamie said sternly.

Dulcy's face fell. "I ain't laughing," she said. "I'm scared. Johnny's going to kill him."

Mamie went rigid. Moments passed before she spoke. Her voice was hushed from fear.

"Did he tell you that?"

"He ain't had to. But I know it. I can feel it."

Mamie stood up and put her arm about Dulcy. Both of them were trembling.

"We got to stop him somehow, child."

Dulcy twisted about to face the mirror again, as though seeking courage from her looks. She opened her pink straw handbag and began repairing her make-up. Her hand trembled as she painted her mouth.

"I don't know how to stop him," she said when she'd finished. "Without my dropping dead."

Mamie took her arm from about Dulcy's waist and wrung her hands involuntarily.

"Lord, I wish Val would hurry up and get here."

Dulcy glanced at her wrist watch.

"It's already four-twenty-five. Johnny ought to be here now himself." After a moment she added, "I don't know what's keeping Val."

3

SOME ONE BEGAN hammering loudly on the door.

The sound was scarcely heard above the din inside the room.

"*Open the door!*" a voice screamed.

It was so loud that even Dulcy and Mamie heard it through the locked bathroom door.

"Wonder who that can be," Mamie said.

"It sure ain't neither Johnny or Val making all that fuss," Dulcy replied.

"Probably some drunk."

One of the drunks already on the inside said in a minstrel man's voice, "Open de do', Richard."

That was the title of a popular song in Harlem that had originated with two blackface comedians on the Apollo theatre stage doing a skit about a colored brother coming home drunk and trying to get Richard to let him into the house.

The other drunks on the inside laughed.

Alamena had just stepped into the kitchen. "See who's at the door," she said to Baby Sis.

Baby Sis looked up from her chore of washing dishes and said sulkily, "All these drunks make me sick."

Alamena froze. Baby Sis was just a girl whom Mamie had taken in to help about the house, and had no right to criticize the guests.

"Girl, you're getting beside yourself," she said. "You'd better mind how you talk. Go open the door and then get this mess cleaned up in here."

Baby Sis looked sidewise about the disordered kitchen, her slant eyes looking evil in her greasy black face.

The table, sink, sidestands and most of the available floor space were strewn with empty and half-filled bottles —gin, whisky and rum bottles, pop bottles, condiment bottles; pots, pans and platters of food, a dishpan containing leftover potato salad, deep iron pots with soggy pieces of fried chicken, fried fish, fried pork chops; baking pans with mashed and mangled biscuits, pie pans with single slices of runny pies; a washtub containing bits of ice floating about in trashy water; slices of cake and spongy white-bread sandwiches, half eaten, lying everywhere— on the tables, sink and floor.

"Ain't never gonna get this mess cleaned up nohow," she complained.

"Git, girl," Alamena said harshly.

Baby Sis shoved her way through the mob of crying drunks in the packed sitting room.

"Somebody open this door!" the voice yelled desperately from outside.

"I'm coming!" Baby Sis shouted from inside. "Keep your pants on."

"Hurry up then!" the voice shouted back.

"Baby, it's cold outside," one of the drunks inside cracked.

Baby Sis stopped in front of the locked door and shouted, "Who is you who been beating on this door like you tryna bust it down?"

"I'm Reverend Short," the voice replied.

"I'm the Queen of Sheba," Baby Sis said, doubling over laughing and beating her big strong thighs. She turned to the guests to let them share the joke. "He say he's Reverend Short."

Several of the guests laughed as though they were stone, raving crazy.

Baby Sis turned around toward the closed door again and shouted, "Try again, Buster, and don't tell me you is Saint Peter coming for Big Joe."

The three musicians kept riffing away in dead-pan trances, their fixed eyes staring from petrified faces into the Promised Land across the river Jordan.

"I tell you I am Reverend Short," the voice said.

Baby Sis's laughing expression went abruptly evil and malevolent.

"You want to know how I know you ain't Reverend Short?"

"That's exactly what I would like to know," the voice said exasperatedly.

"Cause Reverend Short is already inside of here," Baby Sis replied triumphantly. "And you can't be Reverend Short, 'cause you is out there."

"Merciful God in heaven," the voice said moaningly. "Give me patience."

But instead of being patient, the hammering commenced again.

Mamie Pullen unlocked the bathroom door and stuck out her head.

"What's happening out there?" she asked, then, seeing Baby Sis standing before the door, she called, "Who's that at the door?"

15

"Some drunk what claim's he's Reverend Short," Baby Sis replied.

"I'm Reverend Short!" the voice outside screamed.

"It can't be Reverend Short," Baby Sis argued.

"What's the matter with you, girl, you drunk?" Mamie said angrily, advancing across the room.

From the kitchen doorway Alamena said, "It's probably Johnny, pulling one of his gags."

Mamie reached the door, pushed Baby Sis aside and flung it inward.

Reverent Short stepped across the threshold, tottering as though barely able to stand. His parchment-colored bony face was knotted with an expression of extreme outrage, and his reddish eyes glinted furiously behind the polished, gold-rimmed spectacles.

"Hush my mouth!" Baby Sis exclaimed in an awed voice, her black greasy face graying and her bulging eyes whitening as though she'd seen a ghost. "It is Reverend Short."

Reverend Short's thin, black-clad body shook with fury like a sapling in a gale.

"I told you I was Reverend Short," he sputtered.

He had a mouth shaped like that of a catfish, and when he talked he sprayed spit over Dulcy, who had come over to stand with her arm about Mamie's shoulder.

She drew back angrily and wiped her face with the tiny black silk handkerchief that she held in her hand and that represented her dress of mourning.

"Quit spitting on me," she said harshly.

"He didn't mean to spit on you, honey," Mamie said soothingly.

"Po' sinner stands a-trembling . . ." Deep South shouted.

Reverend Short's body twitched convulsively, as though he were having a fit. Everyone stared at him curiously.

". . . stands a-trembling, Daddy Joe," Susie Q. echoed.

"Mamie Pullen, if you don't stop those devils from jamming that sweet old spiritual, *Steal Away,* I swear before God I won't preach Big Joe's funeral," Reverend Short threatened in a rage-croaking voice.

"They're just trying to show their gratitude." Mamie shouted to make herself heard. "It was Big Joe who

16

started them on their way to fame when they was just hustling tips in Eddy Price's joint, and now they're just trying to send him on his way to heaven."

"That ain't no way to send a body to heaven," he said hoarsely, his voice giving out from shouting. "They're making enough noise to wake up the dead who're already there."

"Oh, all right, I'll stop' em," Mamie said, and went over and put her black wrinkled hand on Deep South's dripping wet shoulder. "That's been fine, boys, but you can rest a while now."

The music stopped so suddenly it caught Dulcy whispering angrily—"Why do you let that store-front preacher run your business, Aunt Mamie—" in a sudden pool of silence.

Reverent Short turned a look on her that glinted with malevolence.

"You'd better dust off your own skirts before criticizing me, Sister Perry," he croaked.

The silence became weighted.

Baby Sis chose that moment to say in a loud drunken voice, "What I want to know, Reverend Short, is how in the world did you get outside that door?"

The tension broke. Everyone laughed.

"I was pushed out of the bedroom window," Reverend Short said in a voice that was sticky with evil.

Baby Sis doubled over, started to laugh, caught sight of Reverend Short's face and chopped it off in the middle of the first guffaw.

The others who had started to laugh stopped abruptly. Dead silence dropped like a shroud over the revelry. The guests stared at the Reverend Short in pop-eyed wonder. Their faces wanted to continue laughing, but their minds pulled the reins. On the one hand, the expression of suppressed vindictiveness on Reverend Short's face could easily be that of a man who'd been pushed out of a window. But on the other hand, his body didn't show the effects of a three-story fall to the concrete sidewalk.

"Chink Charlie did it," Reverend Short croaked.

Mamie gasped. "What!"

"You kidding or joking?" Alamena said harshly.

17

Baby Sis was the first to recover. She laughed experimentally and gave Reverend Short an appreciative push.

"You takes the cake, Reverend," she said.

Reverend Short clutched her arm to keep from falling.

She grinned the imbecilic admiration of one practical joker for another.

Mamie turned in a squall of fury and slapped her face.

"You get yourself right straight back to that kitchen," she said sternly. "And don't you dast drink another drop of likker tonight."

Baby Sis's face puckered up like a dried prune and she began blubbering. She was a big strong-bodied mule-like young woman, and crying gave her an expression of pure idiocy. She turned to run back to the kitchen but stumbled over a foot and fell drunkenly to the floor. No one paid her any attention because, with her support withdrawn, Reverend Short began to fall.

Mamie clutched him by the arm and helped him into an armchair. "You just set right there, Reverend, and tell me what happened," she said.

He clutched his left side as though in great pain and croaked in a breathless voice, "I went into the bedroom to get a breath of fresh air, and while I was standing in the window watching a policeman chasing a thief, Chink Charlie sneaked up behind me and pushed me out of the window."

"My God!" Mamie exclaimed. "Then he was trying to kill you."

"Of course he was."

Alamena looked down at the twitching bony face of Reverend Short and said in a reassuring tone, "Mamie, he's just drunk."

"I'm not the least bit drunk," he denied. "I've never drunk a drop of intoxicating liquor in my life."

"Where's Chink?" Mamie asked, looking about. "Chink!" she called. "Somebody get Chink in here."

"He's gone," Alamena said. "He left while you and Dulcy were in the crapper."

"Your preacher's just making that up, Aunt Mamie," Dulcy said. "Just 'cause him and Chink had an argument 'bout the guests you got here."

Mamie looked from her to Reverend Short. "What's wrong with 'em?"

She intended the question for Reverend Short, but Dulcy answered. "He said there shouldn't be nobody here but church members and Big Joe's lodge brothers, and Chink told him he was forgetting that Big Joe was a gambler himself."

"I'm not saying that Big Joe didn't sin," Reverend Short said in his loud pulpit voice, forgetting for the moment he was an invalid. "But Big Joe was a dining-car cook on the Pennsylvania Railroad for more than twenty years, and he was a member of The First Holy Roller Church of Harlem, and that's how God sees him."

"But these folks here is all his friends," Mamie protested with a look of bewilderment. "Folks who worked with him and saw him all the time."

Reverend Short pursed his lips. "That ain't the point. You can't surround his poor soul with all manner of sin and adultery and expect God to take it to his bosom."

"Jus' what do you mean by that?" Dulcy challenged hotly.

"Let him alone," Mamie said. "Everything has done gone bad enough without all this argument."

"If he don't stop picking at me with his dirty hints all the time I'm gonna have Johnny whip his ass," Dulcy said in a low grating voice intended only for Mamie, but everyone heard her.

Reverend Short gave her a look of triumphant malevolence.

"Threaten all you want, you Jezebel, but you can't hide it from the Lord that it was your own devilishness that drove Joe Pullen to an early death."

"That just ain't so," Mamie Pullen contradicted. "It was just his time. He's been taking naps like that, with his cigar in his mouth, for years, and it was just his time that he happened to swallow it and choke to death."

"If you want to put up with this chicken-season preacher's lying, you can," Dulcy said to Mamie. "But I'm going home, and you can just tell Johnny why when he gets here."

Silence followed her as she turned and walked from the apartment. She slammed the door behind her.

Mamie sighed. "Lord, I wish Val was here."

"This house is full of murderers!" Reverend Short exclaimed.

"You shouldn't say that just because you've got a grudge against Chink Charlie," Mamie said.

"For Christ's sake, Mamie!" Alamena exploded. "If he'd fallen from your bedroom window he'd be lying out there on the sidewalk dead."

Reverend Short stared at her through glazed eyes. A white froth had collected in the corners of his mouth.

"I see a terrible vision," he muttered.

"That ain't no lie," Alamena said disgustedly. "All you is seeing is visions."

"I see a dead man stabbed in the heart," he said.

"Let me fix you a toddy and put you to bed," Mamie said soothingly. "And, Alamena—"

"He don't need no more to drink," Alamena cut her off.

"For Jesus Christ's sake, Alamena, stop it. Go phone Doctor Ramsey and tell him to come over here."

"He's not sick," Alamena said.

"I didn't say I was sick," Reverend Short said.

"He's just trying to stir up trouble for some reason."

"I'm hurt," Reverend Short stated. "You'd be hurt, too, if somebody had pushed you out of a window."

Mamie took Alamena by the arm and tried to pull her away. "Go now and telephone the doctor."

But Alamena pulled back. "Listen, Mamie Pullen, for God's sake be your age. If he fell out of that window it's a cinch he couldn't have walked back upstairs. I suppose he's going to tell you next that he fell into the lap of God."

"I fell into a basket of bread," Reverend Short declared.

At last the guests laughed with relief. Now they knew the good reverend was joking. Even Mamie couldn't restrain herself.

"See what I mean?" Alamena said.

"Reverend Short, shame on you, pulling our leg like that," Mamie said indulgently.

"If you don't believe me, go look at the bread," Reverend Short challenged.

"What bread?"

"The basket of bread I fell into. It's on the sidewalk in front of the A&P store. God put it there to break my fall."

Mamie and Alamena exchanged glances.

"I'll go look, you go call the doctor," Mamie said.

"I want to look, too."

Everybody wanted to look.

Sighing loudly, as though indulging the whims of a lunatic against her better judgement, Mamie led the way.

The bedroom door was closed. When she opened it, she exclaimed, "Why, the light's on!"

With growing trepidation she crossed the lighted bedroom and leaned out of the open window. Alamena leaned out beside her. The others squeezed into the medium-sized room. As many as could peered over the two women's shoulders.

"Is it there?" someone in back asked.

"Does they see it?"

"There's a basket of some kind, sure enough," Alamena said.

"But it don't look like it's no bread in it," the man peering over her shoulder said.

"It don't even look like a bread basket," Mamie said, trying to penetrate the early morning shadows with her near-sighted gaze. "It looks like one of them wicker baskets they take away dead bodies in."

By then Alamena's sharp vision had become accustomed to the dark.

"It's a bread basket, all right. But there's a man already lying in it."

"A drunk," Mamie said in a voice of relief. "No doubt that's what Reverend Short saw that gave him the idea of fooling us."

"He don't look drunk to me," said the man who was leaning over her shoulder. "He's lying too straight, and drunks always lay crooked."

"My God!" Alamena exclaimed in a fear-stricken voice. "He's got a knife sticking in him."

21

Mamie let out a long moaning keen. "Lord, protect us, can you see his face, child? I'm getting so old I can't see a lick. Is it Chink?"

Alamena put her arm about Mamie's waist and slowly pulled her from the window.

"No, it ain't Chink," she said. "It looks to me like Val."

4

EVERYONE RUSHED TOWARD the outside door to be the first downstairs. But before Mamie and Alamena could get out the telephone began to ring.

"Who in the hell could that be at this hour?" Alamena said roughly.

"You go ahead, I'll answer it," Mamie said.

Alamena went on without replying.

Mamie went back into the bedroom and lifted the receiver of the telephone on the nightstand beside the bed.

"Hello."

"Are you Mrs. Pullen?" a muffled voice asked. It was so blurred she could scarcely distinguish the words.

"Yes."

"There's a dead man out in front of your house."

She could have sworn the voice held a note of laughter.

"Who are you?" she asked suspiciously.

"I ain't nobody."

"It ain't so goddam funny that you got to make a joke about it," she said roughly.

"I ain't joking. If you don't believe me, go to the window and take a look."

"Why the hell didn't you call the police?"

"I reckoned that maybe you wouldn't want them to know."

Suddenly the whole conversation stopped making sense to Mamie. She tried to collect her thoughts, but she was so tired her head buzzed. And all this monkey business of Reverend Short's, and then Val's getting stabbed to death with Big Joe lying dead there in the coffin, left her feeling as though she had stepped off the edge of sanity.

"Why the hell wouldn't I want the police to know?" she asked savagely.

"Because he came from your apartment."

"How do you know he came from my apartment? I ain't seen him in my house tonight."

"I did. I saw him fall out of your window."

"What? Oh, you're talking about Reverend Short. And you sure enough seen him fall?"

"That's what I'm telling you. And he's lying down on the sidewalk in the A&P bread basket, dead as all hell."

"That ain't Reverend Short. He didn't even get hurt. He come back upstairs."

The voice didn't say anything, so she went on. "It's Val. Valentine Haines. And he was stabbed to death."

She waited for an answer, but the voice still didn't speak.

"Hello," she said. "Hello! You still there! You're so goddam smart how come you didn't see that?"

She heard a very soft click.

"The bastard hung up," she mumbled to herself, then added, "Now if that ain't almighty strange—"

She stood still for a moment, trying to think, but her mind wouldn't work. Then she crossed to the dressing table and picked up a can of snuff. Using a cotton dauber, she dipped a lipful, leaving the dauber in the pocket of her lip with the stick protruding. It quieted her growing sense of panic. Out of respect for her guests, she hadn't taken a dip all night, and as a rule she lived with a dip in her lip.

"Lord, if Big Joe was alive, he'd know what to do," she said to herself as she went with slow, dragging steps back into the sitting room.

It was littered with dirty glasses and plates containing scraps of food, ashtrays overflowing with smoldering cigarette and cigar butts. The maroon-carpeted floor was a mess. Burning cigarettes had left holes in the upholstery, burned scars on the tabletops. The ashy skeleton of a cigarette lay intact atop the grand piano. There was a resemblance to a fairground after a circus has gone, and the smell of death and lilies of the valley and man-made stink was overpowering in the hot, close room.

Mamie dragged herself across the room and looked down into the bronze-painted coffin at the body of her late husband.

Big Joe was dressed in a cream-colored Palm Beach suit, pale green crepe de Chine shirt, brown silk tie with hand-painted angels held in place by a diamond horseshoe stickpin. His big square dark-brown face was clean shaven, with deep creases encircling the wide mouth. It looked freshly massaged. His eyes were closed. His stiff gray kinky hair had been cut short after death and had been painstakingly combed and brushed. She had done it herself, and she had dressed him, too. His hands were folded across his chest, exhibiting a diamond ring on his left hand and his lodge signet ring on his right.

She removed all of the jewelry and put it down into the deep front pocket of her long black satin Mother Hubbard dress that swept the floor. Then she closed the coffin.

"One hell of a wake this turned out to be," she said.

"He's dead," Reverend Short said suddenly in his new croaking voice.

Mamie gave a start. She hadn't seen Reverend Short.

He sat slouched on the end of his spine in an overstuffed armchair, staring with a fixed expression toward the opposite wall.

"What the hell do you think," she said roughly. All her social affections had left since the discovery of Val's body. "You think I'd bury him if he was alive?"

"I saw it happen," Reverend Short continued as though she hadn't spoken.

She stared at him in perplexity. "Oh, you mean Val."

"A woman filled with the sin of lust and adultery came from the pit of hell and stabbed him in the heart."

His words sunk slowly into Mamie's clogged thoughts.

"A woman?"

"And I gave her space to repent of her fornication, and she repented not."

"You saw her do it?"

24

*"For her sins have reached unto heaven, and God hath
remembered her iniquities."*

Mamie saw the room tilt.

"May the Lord have mercy," she said.

She saw Big Joe in his coffin, the grand piano and the
console radio-television set begin a slow ascent toward
heaven. Then the dark maroon carpet rose slowly until it
spread out before her eyes like a sea of dark, congealed
blood into which she buried her face.

"Sin and lust and abomination in the sight of the Lord,"
Reverend Short croaked, then added in a small dry
whisper, "She ain't nothing but a whore, O Lord."

5

THE AUTOMATIC ELEVATOR was on the ground floor,
and most of the curious mourners chose to run down
the stairs rather than wait for it. But they were not the
first to arrive.

Dulcy and Chink stood facing each other across the
basket of bread containing the body. He was a big yellow
man, young but going to fat, dressed in a beige summer
suit. He leaned over tensely.

The first to approach heard Dulcy exclaiming, "Jesus
Christ, you didn't have to kill him!" and Chink replying
in a voice choked with sudden passion, "Not even for
you—" Then he broke off and cautioned in a tense
whisper, speaking between set lips, "Shut up and play it
dumb."

She didn't speak again until all the mourners from the
wake had gathered and had their look and said their say.

"It's Val, and he's dead all right."

"If he ain't, Saint Peter's going to be mighty surprised."

Alamena had wormed close enough to get a clear view
of the body. She heard a dining-car waiter say, "You
reckon he was stabbed where he's at?"

A voice behind her replied, "Must have been—there ain't no blood nowhere else."

The body lay at full length on the mattress of soft wrapped loaves of bread as though the basket had been fitted to its measure. The left hand, exhibiting the band of a single gold ring, lay palm upward across a heavy, black silk knitted tie knotted about the collar of a soft sand-colored linen silk shirt; the right hand lay palm downward across the center button of the jacket of an olive drab sheen gabardine suit. The feet pointed straight up, exposing the slightly worn crepe-rubber soles of lightweight Cordovan English-made shoes.

The knife protruded from the jacket just beneath the breast pocket, which was adorned with a quarter-inch stripe of white handkerchief. It was a stag-handle knife with a push-button opener and handguard, such as used by hunters to skin game.

Blood made irregular patterns over the jacket, shirt and tie. Splotches were on the waxed-paper wrappings of the loaves of bread, and on one side of the woven rattan basket. There was none on the sidewalk.

The face was set in a fixed expression of utter disbelief; the eyes, widened into protruding white-rimmed balls, stared fixedly at some point above and beyond the feet.

It was a handsome face, with smooth brown skin and features bearing a close resemblance to Dulcy's. The head was bare, revealing curly black hair, thickly plastered with pomade.

An odd moment of silence followed the last speaker's statement as the fact sunk in that the murder had been committed on the spot.

Dulcy said into the silence, "He looks so surprised."

"You'd look surprised, too, if some one stuck a knife in your heart," Alamena said grimly.

With a startling abruptness, Dulcy became hysterical.

"Val!" she screamed. "I'll get him, Val, sugar, oh God—"

She would have thrown herself atop Val's body, but Alamena quickly wrenched her away, and several of the mourners closed in and held her.

She struggled furiously and screamed, "Turn me loose,

26

you mother-rapers! He's my brother and some mother-raper's going to pay—"

"For Jesus sake, shut up!" Alamena shouted.

Chink stared at her, his big yellow face distorted with rage. She shut up and got herself under control.

A colored patrolman came from the doorway of the adjoining building. When he saw the crowd he drew himself up and began adjusting his uniform.

"What's happened here?" he asked in a loud self-conscious voice. "Somebody get hurt?"

"You can call it that," some one replied.

The patrolman pushed in close and looked down at the body. The collar of his blue uniform was open, and he smelled like sweat.

"Who stabbed him?" he asked.

Pigmeat replied in a high falsetto voice, "Don't you wish you knew."

The patrolman blinked his eyes, then suddenly grinned, showing rows of big yellow teeth.

"What minstrel you with, sonny-o?"

Everyone stared at him, waiting to see what he would do. Their faces took dark shape in the graying light of dawn.

He stood there grinning, doing nothing. He didn't know what to do, but he wasn't perturbed by it.

The distant sound of a siren floated in the humid air. The crowd began to scatter.

"Don't nobody leave the scene," the patrolman ordered.

The red eye of a patrol car came north up Seventh Avenue. The patrol car made a screaming U-turn around the park dividing the traffic lanes and dragged to a stop, double-parking beside the cars at the curb. Another red eye was coming south down the dark street in a screaming fury. A third turned the corner of 132nd Street, almost colliding with it. A fourth turned in from 129th Street and screamed north on the wrong side of the avenue.

The white precinct sergeant arrived in the fifth patrol car.

"Keep everybody here," he ordered in a loud voice.

By then half-clad people were hanging from every front

27

window in the block, and others began collecting in the street.

The sergeant noticed a white man clad in a short-sleeved white sport shirt and khaki trousers standing apart, and asked him, "Do you work in this A&P store?"

"I'm the manager."

"Open it up. We're going to put these suspects inside."

"I object," the white man said. "I've been robbed once tonight by a shine, right under my eyes, and the cop hasn't even caught the thief."

The sergeant looked at the colored cop.

"It was his buddy," the A&P manager said.

"Where is he now?" the sergeant asked.

"How in the hell do I know?" the store manager replied. "I had to leave and come back to open the store."

"Well, go ahead and open it," the colored cop said.

"I'll be responsible if anything is stolen," the sergeant said.

The manager went to unlock the door without replying.

An inconspicuous black sedan pulled to the curb and parked at the end of the block unnoticed, and two tall, lanky colored men dressed in black mohair suits that looked as though they'd been slept in got out and walked back toward the scene. Their wrinkled coats bulged beneath their left shoulders. The shiny straps of their shoulder holsters showed across the fronts of their blue cotton shirts.

The one with the burnt face went to the far side of the crowd; the other remained on the near side.

Suddenly a loud voice shouted, "Straighten up!"

An equally loud voice echoed, "Count off!"

"Detectives Grave Digger Jones and Coffin Ed Johnson reporting for duty, General," Pigmeat muttered.

"Jesus Christ!" Chink fumed. "Now we've got those damned Wild West gunmen here to mess up everything."

The sergeant said, winking at a white cop, "Herd 'em into the store, Jones, you and Johnson. You fellows know how to handle 'em."

Grave Digger gave him a hard look. "They all look alike to us, Commissioner—white, blue, black and me-

28

rino." Then turning to the crowd he shouted, "Inside, cousins."

"They're going to hold prayer meeting," Coffin Ed said.

As the cops were closing the door on the corraled suspects, a big cream-colored, made-to-order Cadillac convertible with the top down stopped in the street, double-parking behind the row of patrol cars.

A small white-faced playing card was embossed on each door. In the corners of each card were an inlaid spade, heart, diamond and club. Each door was the size of a barn gate.

One of the doors swung open. A man got out. He was a big man but, standing, his six-foot height lost impressiveness in his slanting shoulders and long arms. He was wearing a powder blue suit of shantung silk; a pale yellow crepe silk shirt; a hand-painted tie depicting an orange sun rising on a dark blue morning; highly glossed light tan rubber-soled shoes; a miniature ten-of-hearts tie pin with opal hearts; three rings, including a heavy gold signet ring of his lodge, a yellow diamond set in a heavy gold band and a big mottled stone of a nameless variety, also set in a heavy gold band. His cuff links were heavy gold squares with diamond eyes. It wasn't from vanity he wore so much gold. He was a gambler, and it was his bank account in any emergency.

He was bareheaded. His kinky hair, powdered with gray, was cut as short as a three-days' growth of whiskers, with a part shaved on one side. In the dim light of morning his big-featured, knotty face showed it had taken its lumps. In the center of his forehead was a puffed, bluish scar with ridges pronging off like immobilized octopus tentacles. It gave him an expression of perpetual rage, which was accentuated by the smoldering fire that lay always just beneath the surface of his muddy brown eyes, ready to flame into a blaze.

He looked hard, strong, tough and unafraid.

"Johnny Perry!"

The name came involuntarily to the lips of everyone who lived in Harlem. "He's the greatest," they said.

Dulcy waved to him from inside the store.

He walked toward the cops who were congregated

29

about the door. His step was springy, and he walked on the balls of his feet like a prize fighter. A wave of nervous motion stirred among the cops.

"What's the rumble" he asked the sergeant.

For an instant no one spoke.

Then the sergeant said, nodding toward the bread basket on the sidewalk, "Man's been killed," as though the words had been forced from him by the quick hot flame that began to flicker in Johnny's eyes.

Johnny turned his head to look, then walked over and stared down at Val's body. He stood as though frozen for almost a minute. When he walked back his dark face had taken on a deep purple tint, and the tentacles of the scar on his forehead seemed to have come alive. His eyes had the hot steamy glow of water-logged wood beginning to burn.

But his voice had the same slow, deep, gambler's pitch that never changed.

"Do you know who stuck him?"

The sergeant gave him back look for look. "Not yet. Do you?"

Johnny put his left hand forward, fingers stiff and splayed, then drew it in and stuck it into his coat pocket, the same as his other hand. He did not reply.

Dulcy had wormed between the displays close enough to the plate-glass to rap on it.

Johnny threw her a look, then said to the sergeant, "You got my old lady in there. Let her out."

"She's a suspect," the sergeant said tonelessly.

"It's her brother," Johnny said.

"You can see her at the station. The wagons will be here soon," the sergeant replied indifferently.

The flames leaped up in Johnny's muddy eyes.

"Let her out," Grave Digger said. "He'll bring her in."

"Who in the God-damned hell's going to bring him in?" the sergeant raved.

"We'll bring him in," Grave Digger said. "Me and Ed."

The first of the wagons turned the corner into Seventh Avenue. The sergeant opened the door and said, "All right, let's start getting them out."

Dulcy was the third in line. She had to wait until the

30

cops shook down the two men in front of her. One of the cops asked her to hand over her pocketbook, but she ran past him and flew into Johnny's arms.

"Oh Johnny," she sobbed, staining the front of his powder blue silk suit with lipstick, mascara and tears as she buried her face in his chest.

He embraced her with a tenderness that seemed startling in a man of his appearance.

"Don't cry, baby," he said in his changeless voice, "I'll get the mother-raper."

"Youd better get into the wagon," a white patrol cop said, approaching Dulcy. Grave Digger gestured him back.

Johnny escorted Dulcy toward his parked Cadillac convertible as though she were an invalid.

When Alamena came out, she stepped from line, walked quickly to the Cadillac and got in beside Dulcy.

No one said anything to her.

Johnny started the motor, but was held up for a moment by a car from the coroner's office that had stopped in front of him. The assistant coroner got out with his black bag and walked toward the body. Two cops came from the apartment entrance with Mamie Pullen and Reverend Short.

"Over here," Alamena called.

"Thank God," Mamie said. She made her way slowly between the parked cars and climbed into the back seat.

"There's room for you too, Reverend Short," Alamena called.

"I'll not ride with a murderer," he replied in his croaking voice, and went tottering toward the second of the wagons that had just pulled up.

The eyes of every cop went quickly from his face toward the occupants of the cream-colored Cadillac.

"Take your curse off me!" Dulcey screamed, becoming hysterical again.

"Shut up!" Alamena said harshly.

Johnny shifted into drive without looking around, and the big shiny car moved slowly off. The small black battered sedan bearing Coffin Ed and Grave Digger followed close behind.

6

THE PRELIMINARY QUESTIONING was made by another sergeant, Detective Sergeant Brody from dowtown Homicide, with the precinct detectives, Grave Digger Jones and Coffin Ed Johnson, assisting.

The questioning was conducted in a soundproof room without windows on the first floor. This room was known to the Harlem underworld as the "Pigeon Nest." It was said that no matter how tough an egg was, if they kept him in there long enough he would hatch out a pigeon.

The room was lit by the hot bright glare of a three-hundred-watt spotlight focused on a low wooden stool bolted to the boards in the center of the bare wooden floor. The seat of the stool was shiny from the squirming of countless suspects who had sat on it.

Sergeant Brody sat with his elbows propped atop a big battered flat-topped desk that stood along the inner wall beside the door. The desk was beyond the edge of shadow that screened the interrogator from the suspects sizzling in the glaring light.

At one end of the desk, a police reporter sat in a straight-backed chair with his notebook on the desk in front of him.

Coffin Ed made a tall indistinct shadow in the corner behind.

Grave Digger stood at the other end of the desk, his foot propped on the one remaining chair. Both had kept on their hats.

The principals—Val's friends and intimates, Johnny and Dulcy Perry, Mamie Pullen, Reverend Short and Chink Charlie—were being held upstairs in the detective bureau for the last.

The others had been herded into the bull pen downstairs and were brought out four at a time and lined abreast in the circle of light.

The sight of the corpse and the subsequent ride in the wagon had sobered them too suddenly. They were sweaty and evil, men and women alike, their haggard, vari-colored faces looking like African war masks in the dead white light.

After their names, addresses and occupations had been taken, Sergeant Brody asked them routine questions in a passionless copper's voice:

"Were there any arguments at the wake? Fights? Did any of you hear anyone mention Valentine Haines's name? Did any of you see Chink Charlie Dawson leave the room? What time? Was he alone? Did Doll Baby leave with him? Before? After?

"Did any of you see Reverend Short leave the house? Leave the sitting room? Go into the bedroom? Did you notice whether the bedroom door was open or closed most of the evening? How much time elapsed between the time he disappeared until his return?

"Did any of you notice Dulcy Perry leave the house? Before or after Reverend Short returned?

"How much time elapsed between Reverend Short's return and when all of you went to the window to look for the bread basket? Five minutes? More? Less? Did anyone else leave during that time? Do any of you know if Val had any enemies? Anyone who might have had a grudge against him? Was he in any kind of trouble?"

There were seven men in the pickup who hadn't been at the wake. Brody asked if they'd seen anyone fall from the third-story-front window; if they'd seen anyone passing along the street, walking or in a car. None admitted seeing anything. All swore that they'd been inside of their homes, in bed, and had gone out on the street after the patrol cars arrived.

"Did any of you hear anyone cry out?" Brody asked. "Hear the sound of a car passing? Any strange sound of any kind?"

His questions all drew negatives.

"All right, all right," he growled. "All of you were in bed, sleeping the sleep of the righteous, dreaming about

33

the angels in heaven—you didn't see anything, didn't hear anything, and you don't know anything. All right . . ."

All were asked to identify the murder knife, which Brody exhibited to each group. None did.

In between the questions and the answers, the stylo of the police reporter was heard scratching on sheet after sheet of foolscap paper.

The contents of each person's pockets had been dumped on top of the desk as each group was ushered in. The sergeant examined only the knives. When the blades exceeded the two inches allowed by law, he inserted them into the crevice between the top of the center drawer and the desk top and broke them with a slight downward pressure. As time went on broken blades piled up inside the drawer.

When he'd finished with the last group, Brody looked at his watch.

"Two hours and seventeen minutes," he said. "And all I've learned so far is that the folks here in Harlem are so respectable their fingers don't stink."

"What did you expect?" Coffin Ed asked. "For somebody to say they did it?"

"Do you want me to read the transcript?" the police reporter asked.

"Hell no. The coroner's report says the victim was killed where he lay. But nobody saw him arrive. Nobody remembers exactly when Chink Charlie left the flat. Nobody knows when Dulcy Perry left. Nobody knows for certain whether Reverend Short even fell out of the Goddamned window. Do you believe that, Digger?"

"Why not? This is Harlem, where anything can happen."

"We people here in Harlem will believe anything," Coffin Ed said.

"You're not trying to pull my leg, are you, pal?" Brody said dryly.

"I'm just trying to tell you that these people are not so simple as you think," Coffin Ed replied. "You're trying to find the murderer. All right, I'll believe anybody did it if we get enough proof."

"Okay, fine," Brody said. "Bring in Mamie Pullen."

34

When Grave Digger escorted Mamie into the room, he placed the chair he'd been using for a footrest in a comfortable position so she could lean an arm on the desk if she wished, then went over and adjusted the light so it wouldn't bother her.

Sergeant Brody's first glance had taken in the black satin dress with its skirt that dragged the floor, reminiscent of the rigid uniform of whorehouse madams in the 1920's. He'd gotten a peep at the toes of the men's straight-last shoes protruding from beneath. His gaze remained longer on the two-carat diamond in the platinum band encircling her gnarled brown ring finger, and rested for an appreciable time on the white jade necklace that dropped to her waist like a greatly cherished rosary with a black onyx cross attached to the end. Then he looked at the old brown face, lined with grief and worry, sagging in loose folds beneath the tight knot of short, straightened, gray-streaked hair.

"This is Sergeant Brody, Aunt Mamie," Grave Digger said. "He must ask you a few questions."

"How do you do, Mr. Brody," she said, sticking her gnarled unadorned right hand across the desk.

"It's a bad business, Mrs. Pullen," the sergeant said, shaking her hand.

"It looks like one death always calls for another," she said. "Been that way ever since I could remember. One person dies and then there ain't no end. I guess that's the way God planned it."

Then she looked up to see the face of the cop who had been so gentle with her, and exclaimed, "Lord bless my soul, you're little Digger Jones. I've known you ever since you were a little shavetail kid on 116th Street. I didn't know you were the one they called Grave Digger."

Grave Digger grinned sheepishly, like a little boy caught stealing apples.

"I've grown up now, Aunt Mamie."

"Doesn't time fly. As Big Joe always used to say; *Tempers fugits.* You must be all of thirty-five years old now."

"Thirty-six. And here's Eddy Johnson, too. He's my partner."

Coffin Ed stepped forward into the light. Mamie was stunned at sight of his face.

"God in heaven!" she exclaimed involuntarily. "What hap—" then caught herself.

"A hoodlum threw a glass of acid in my face." He shrugged. "Occupational hazard, Aunt Mamie. I'm a cop. I take my chances."

She apologized. "Now I remember reading about it, but I didn't know it was you. I hardly ever go anywhere, but just out with Big Joe, when he was alive." Then she added with sincerity, "I hope they put whoever did it in the jail and throw away the key."

"He's already buried, Aunt Mamie," Coffin Ed said.

Then Grave Digger said, "Ed's having skin grafted on his face from his thigh, but it takes time. It'll take about a year altogether before it's finished."

"Now, Mrs. Pullen," the sergeant inserted firmly, "suppose you just tell me in your own words what happened in your place last night, or rather this morning."

She sighed. "I'll tell you what I know."

When she'd finished her account, the sergeant said, "Well, at least that gives us a pretty clear picture of what actually happened inside of your house from the time Reverend Short returned upstairs until the body was discovered.

"Do you believe that Reverend Short fell from your bedroom window?"

"Oh, I believe that. There wasn't reason for him to say he'd fallen if he hadn't. 'Sides which, he was outside and nobody had seen him leave by the door."

"You don't think that's extraordinary? For him to fall out of a third-story window?"

"Well, sir, he's a frail man and given to having trances. He might have had a trance."

"Epilepsy?"

"No, sir, just religious trances. He sees visions."

"What kind of visions?"

"Oh, all kinds of visions. He preaches about them. He's a prophet, like Saint John the Divine."

Sergeant Brody was a Catholic and he looked bewildered.

36

Grave Digger explained, "Saint John the Divine is the prophet who saw the seven veils and the four horsemen of the apocalypse. The people here in Harlem have a great regard for Saint John. He was the only prophet who ever saw any winning numbers in his visions."

"The *Revelation* is the fortune teller's Bible," Coffin Ed added.

"It's not only just that," Mamie said. "Saint John saw how wonderful it was in heaven and how terrible it was in hell."

"Well now, to get back to this murder, would Chink Charlie have any reason to try to kill Reverend Short?" Brody questioned. "Other than the fact the Reverend was a prophet."

"No, sir, absolutely not. It was just that Reverend Short had the sense knocked out of him by his fall and didn't know what he was saying."

"But he and Chink had been arguing earlier."

"Not really arguing. Reverend Short and him was just disagreeing about the kind of people I had to the wake. But it weren't neither one of them's business."

"Is there bad blood between Dulcy and Reverend Short?"

"Bad blood? No, sir. It's just that Reverend Short thinks Dulcy needs saving and she just takes every chance to bitch him off. But I suspects he's carrying a secret torch for her, only he's shamed of it 'cause of him being a preacher and she being a married woman."

"How was the Reverend with Johnny and Val?"

"They all three respected one another's intentions and that's as far as it went."

"How long was it between the time Dulcy left the house and you went to the window and discovered the body?"

"It wasn't no time at all," she declared positively. "She hadn't even had time to get downstairs."

He asked a few questions about the other mourners, but found no connection with Val.

The he came in from another angle.

"Did you recognize the voice of the man who telephoned you after the body was discovered?"

"No, sir. It just sounded distant and fuzzy."

"But whoever it was knew there was a dead body there in that bread basket?"

"No, sir, it was just like I told you before. Whoever it was wasn't talking about Val. He was talking about Reverend Short. He'd seen the reverend fall and thought he was lying there dead, and that's why he called. I'm sure of that."

"How could he know he was dead unless he had come close enough to examine him?"

"I don't know, sir. I suppose he just thought he was dead. You'd think anybody was dead who'd fallen out a third-story window, and then lay there without getting up."

"But according to testimony, Reverend Short did get up and come all the way back upstairs on his own power."

"Well, I couldn't say how it was. All I know is someone telephoned and when I said he'd been stabbed—Val, I mean—they just hung up as if they might have been surprised."

"Could it have been Johnny Perry?"

"No, sir, I'm dead certain it wasn't him. And I sure ought to know his voice if anybody does, as long as I've been hearing it."

"He's your stepson? Or is it your godson?"

"Well, he ain't rightly neither, but we thought of him as a son because when he came out of stir—"

"What stir? Where?"

"In Georgia. He did a stretch on the chain gang."

"For what?"

"He killed a man for beating his mother—his stepfather. At least she was his common-law wife, his ma, but she was no good and Johnny was always a good boy. They gave him a year on the road."

"When was that?"

"It was twenty-six years ago when he got out. While he was inside his ma ran off with another man and me and Big Joe was coming North. So we just brought him along with us. He was just twenty years old."

"That makes him forty-six now."

"Yes, sir. And Big Joe got him a job on the road."

"Waiting tables?"

"No, sir, helping in the kitchen. He couldn't wait tables on account of that scar."

"How'd he get that?"

"On the chain gang. He and another con got to fighting with pickaxes over a card game. Johnny was always hotheaded, and that con had accused him of cheating him out of a nickel. And Johnny was always as honest as the day is long."

"When did he open his gambling club here?"

"The Tia Juana club? He opened that about ten years ago. Big Joe staked him. But he had another little house-rent game he used to run before that."

"Is that when he married Dulcy—Mrs. Perry—when he opened the Tia Juana club?"

"Oh no-no-no, he just married her a year and a half ago—January second last year, the day after New Year's day. Before then he was married to Alamena."

"Is he married to Dulcy or just living with her?" The sergeant gave her a confidential look.

Her back stiffened. "Their marriage is as legal as whisky. Me and Big Joe were the witnesses. They were married in City Hall."

The sergeant turned a bright fiery red.

Grave Digger said softly, "Couples do get married in Harlem."

Sergeant Brody felt himself on bumpy water and took another tack.

"Does Johnny keep much cash on hand?"

"I don't know, sir."

"In the bank then, or in property? Do you know what property he owns?"

"No, sir. Maybe Big Joe knew, but he never told me."

He dropped it.

"Do you mind telling me what you and Dulcy—Mrs. Perry—were talking about that was so important you had to lock yourself in the bathroom?"

She hesitated and looked appealingly toward Grave Digger.

He said. "We're not after Johnny, Aunt Mamie. This has nothing to do with his gambling club or income taxes or anything concerning the Federal government. We're just trying to find out who killed Val."

"Lord, it's a mystery who'd want to hurt Val. He didn't have an enemy in the world."

The sergeant let that pass. "Then it wasn't Val you and Dulcy were talking about?"

"No, sir. I'd just asked her about a run-in Johnny and Chink had at Dickie Wells's last Saturday night."

"About what? Money? Gambling debts?"

"No, sir. Johnny's crazy jealous of Dulcy—he's going to kill somebody about that gal some day. And Chink imagines he's God's gift to women. He keeps shooting at Dulcy. Folks say he don't mean nothing by it, but—"

"What folks?"

"Well, Val and Alamena and even Dulcy herself. But there ain't no telling what any man means when he keeps after a woman unless it's to get her. And Johnny's so jealous and hot-headed I'm scared to death there's going to be blood trouble."

"What part did Val play in that?"

"Val. He was always just a peacemaker. 'Course, he was on Johnny's side. He spent most of his time, it looked like, just trying to keep Johnny out of trouble. But he didn't have nothing against Chink, either."

"Then Johnny's enemies are his enemies, too?"

"No, sir, I wouldn't say that. Val wasn't the kind of person who had enemies. He and Chink always got along fine."

"Who's Val's woman?"

"He's never had a steady. Not to my knowledge. He just plays the field. I think his latest was Doll Baby. But he wasn't intending to get corralled by no gal."

"Tell me one thing, Mrs. Pullen—didn't you notice anything strange about the body?"

"Well—" She knitted her brows. "Not as I recollect. I didn't get to see him close up, of course. I just saw him from my window. But I didn't notice nothing strange."

The sergeant stared at her.

"Wouldn't you call a knife sticking in his heart strange?"

"Oh, you mean him being stabbed. Yes, sir, I thought

40

that was strange. I couldn't imagine nobody wanting to kill Val."

The sergeant kept staring at her though he didn't quite know what to make of that statement.

"If it had been Johnny there instead of Val it wouldn't have struck you as strange."

"No, sir."

"But didn't it strike you as strange how he came to be lying there in that bread basket just a few minutes after Reverend Short had fallen from your window into the same bread basket?"

For the first time her face took on a look of fear.

"Yes, sir," she replied in a whisper, leaning on the desk for support. "Powerful strange. Only the Lord knows how he came there."

"No, the murderer knows, too."

"Yes, sir. But there's one thing, Mr. Brody. Johnny didn't do it. He might not have had no burning love for his brother-in-law, but he tolerated him on account of Dulcy, and he wouldn't have let nobody hurt a hair on his head, much less have done it hisself."

Brody took the murder knife from a drawer and laid it on the desk top. "Have you ever seen this before?"

She stared at it, more out of curiosity than horror. "No, sir."

He let it drop. "When is the funeral to be held?"

"This afternoon at two o'clock."

"All right, you may go now. You've been a great help to us."

She arose slowly, bracing her hands on the desk top, and extended her hand to Sergeant Brody with Southern-bred courtesy.

Sergeant Brody wasn't used to it. He was the law. People on the other side of this desk were generally on the other side of the law. He found himself so confused that he clambered to his feet, knocking over his chair, and pumped her hand up and down, his face glowing like a freshly boiled lobster.

"I hope your funeral goes well, Mrs. Pullen—that is, I mean, your husband's funeral."

41

"Thank you, sir. All we can do is put him in the ground and hope."

Grave Digger and Coffin Ed stepped forward and escorted her with deference to the door, holding it open for her to pass through. Her black satin dress dragged on the floor, sweeping dust over her straight-last shoes.

Sergeant Brody didn't sigh. He prided himself on the fact that he never sighed. But, as he glanced at his watch again, he looked as though he would have loved to.

"It's ten-twenty. Think we can finish before lunch?"

"Let's get it over with," Coffin Ed said harshly. "I haven't had any sleep and I'm hungry enough to eat dog."

"Let's have the preacher, then."

On catching sight of the shiny wooden stool sitting in the spill of glaring light, Reverend Short drew up just inside the door and shuddered like a stuck sheep.

"No!" he croaked, trying to back out into the corridor. "I won't go in there."

The two uniformed cops who'd brought him from the detention block gripped his arms and forced him inside.

He struggled in their grip, performing exercises like an adagio dancer. Veins roped in his bony temples. His eyes protruded behind his gold-rimmed spectacles like a bug's under a microscope, and his Adam's apple bobbed like a float on a fishing line.

"No! No! It's haunted with the souls of tortured Christians," he screamed.

"Come on, buddy boy, quit performing," one of the cops said, handling him rough. "Ain't no Christians been in here."

"Yes! Yes!" he screamed in his croaking voice. "I hear their cries. It's the chamber of the Inquisition. I smell the blood of the martyred."

"You must be having a nosebleed," the other cop said, trying to be funny.

They lifted him bodily, feet and legs dangling grotesquely like a puppet's from a gibbet, carried him across the floor and deposited him on the stool.

The three inquisitors stared at him without moving. The chair in which Mamie Pullen had sat once more served Grave Digger as a footstool. Coffin Ed had retired to his dark corner.

"Caesars!" he croaked.

The cops stood flanking him, a hand on each shoulder.

"Cardinals!" he screamed. "The Lord is my shepherd, I shall not fear."

His eyes glinted insanely.

Sergeant Brody's face remained impassive, but he said, "Ain't nobody here but us chickens, Reverend."

Reverend Short leaned forward and peered into the shadow as though trying to make out a blurred figure in a thick fog.

"If you're a police officer then I want to report that Chink Charlie pushed me out of the window to my death, but God placed the body of Christ on the ground to break my fall."

"It was a basket of bread," the sergeant corrected.

"The body of Christ," Reverend Short maintained.

"All right, Reverend, let's cut the comedy," Brody said. "If you're trying to build a plea of insanity, you're jumping the gun. No one is accusing you of anything."

"It was that Jezebel Dulcy Perry who stabbed him with the knife Chink Charlie gave her to commit the murder."

Brody leaned forward slightly.

"You saw him give her the knife?"

"Yes."

"When?"

"The day after Christmas. She was sitting in her car outside my church and thought there wasn't nobody looking. He came up and got into the seat beside her, gave her the knife and showed her how to use it."

"Where were you?"

"I was watching through a crack in the window. I knew there was something fishy about her coming to my church to give me some old clothes for charity."

"Were she and Johnny members of your church?"

"They called themselves members just 'cause Big Joe Pullen was a member, but they never come 'cause they don't like to roll."

Grave Digger saw that Brody didn't get it, so he explained. "It's a Holy Roller church. When the members get happy they roll about on the floor."

"With one another's wives," Coffin Ed added.

Brody's face went sort of slack, and the police reporter stopped writing to stare open-mouthed.

"They keep their clothes on," Grave Digger amended. "They just roll about on the floor and have convulsions, singly and in pairs."

The reporter looked disappointed.

"Ahem," Brody said, clearing his throat. "So when you first looked out of the window you saw Val's body lying in the bread basket with the knife sticking in it. And you recognized the knife as the same knife you had seen Chink Charlie give to Dulcy Perry?"

"There wasn't any bread there then," Reverend Short stated.

Sergeant Brody blinked. "What was there if there wasn't any bread?"

"There was a colored cop and a white man chasing a thief."

"Ah, so you saw that," Brody said, finally getting something tangible to put his teeth into. "Then you must have actually seen the murder being committed."

"I saw her stab him," Reverend Short declared.

"You couldn't have seen her because she hadn't left the flat then," Brody said.

"I didn't see it then. I was pushed out of the window then. I didn't see it until after I had returned to the room."

"Returned to what room?"

"The room where the casket was."

Brody stared at him and slowly began to redden. "Listen, Reverend," he warned. "This is serious. This is a murder investigation. This is no place to joke."

"I'm not joking," Reverend Short said.

"All right, then, you mean you imagined all of this?"

Reverend Short straightened his back and stared at Brody indignantly.

"I saw it in a vision."

"And it was in this vision you saw yourself pushed out of the window?"

44

"It was after I was pushed out of the window that I had the vision."

"Do you have these visions often?"

"Regularly, and they're always true."

"All right, then how did she kill him—in your vision, that is?"

"She went downstairs on the elevator, and when she went outside there was Valentine Haines lying in the basket where I had fallen—"

"I thought you said there wasn't any basket?"

"There wasn't at the time, but the body of Christ had turned into a basket of bread, and it was in this bread that he was lying when she took the knife from her pocketbook and went up to him and stabbed him."

"What was Val doing there?"

"He was lying there, waiting for her to come out."

"And stab him, I suppose."

"He didn't expect her to stab him. He didn't even know she had a knife."

"All right. I don't buy any of that. Did you see anyone actually leave the house—that is actually see them—while you were downstairs?"

"My eyes were veiled. I knew a vision was coming on."

"All right, Reverend, I'm going to let you go," Brody said, looking over the contents of Reverend Short's pockets lying on the desk before him. "But for a man who calls himself a minister of the gospel you haven't been very coöperative."

Reverend Short didn't move.

Brody pushed the pocket Bible, handkerchief, bunch of keys and wallet across the desk, hesitated over the bottle of medicine and on sudden impulse drew the cork and smelled it. He looked startled. He tilted it to his lips and tasted it, spat it out on the floor.

"Jesus Christ!" he exclaimed. "Peach brandy and laudanum. You drink this stuff?"

"It's for my nerves," Reverend Short said.

"For your visions, you mean. If I drank this stuff I'd have visions, too." To the cops Brody said disgustedly, "Take him away."

Suddenly Reverend Short began to scream, "Don't let

her get away! Arrest her! Burn her! She's a witch! She's in collusion with the devil! And Chink's her accomplice!"

"We'll take care of her," one of the cops cajoled as they lifted him from the stool. "We've got just the place for witches—and wizards, too, so you'd better look out."

Reverend Short broke from their grasp and fell to the floor. He rolled and threshed about convulsively, frothing at the mouth as though having a fit.

"I see what you mean by Holy Roller," Brody said.

The police reporter snickered.

"No, this is probably a vision coming on," Grave Digger said with a straight face.

Brody looked at him sharply.

The cops picked Reverend Short up by the feet and shoulders and carried him off bodily. After a moment one of them came back for the reverend's possessions.

"Is he crazy or just acting?" Brody asked.

"Maybe both," Grave Digger replied.

"After all, there might be something in what he said," Coffin Ed ventured. "As I recall my Bible, all the prophets were either crazy or epileptic."

"I like some of what he said, all right," Brody admitted. "I just don't like the way he said it."

"Who's next?" Grave Digger asked.

"Let's see Johnny's former wife," Brody said.

Alamena came in docilely, fingering the high-necked collar about her throat, like a girl who might have been in there before and knew what to expect.

She sat down in the circle of light and folded her hands in her lap. She wore no jewelry of any kind.

"What do I call you?" Brody asked.

"Just Alamena," she said.

"Fine. Now just give me a quick fill-in on Val and Dulcy."

"There ain't much to it. Dulcy came here to sing in Small's Cabaret a couple of years ago, and after six months she'd hooked Johnny and landed on easy street. Val came for the wedding and stayed."

"Who were Dulcy's boy friends before she married?"

"She played the field, prospecting."

"How about Val? Was he prospecting, too?"

46

"Why should he? He had a claim staked out for him before he got here."

"He just helped out in the club?" Brody suggested.

"Not so you could notice," she said. "Anyway, Johnny wouldn't have never trusted Val to gamble his money."

"Just what was going on between Dulcy and Chink and Val and Johnny?"

"Nothing, as I know of."

"All right, all right. Who were Val's enemies?"

"He didn't have any enemies. He wasn't the type."

Blood mottled Brody's face.

"God damn it, he didn't stab himself in the heart."

"It's been done before," she said.

"But he didn't. We know that. On the other hand, there were no superficial signs of his being either drugged or drunk. Of course, the coroner can't be absolutely certain until after the autopsy. But let's just imagine he was lying there, at that time of morning, in that basket of bread. Why?"

"Maybe he was standing up and just fell there after he was stabbed."

"No, he was stabbed while he was lying there. And from the condition of the bread he knew absolutely that some one or some thing had already lain in it. Perhaps he had even seen Reverend Short fall from the window. Now I want to ask you just one simple question. Why would he lie there of his own free will, let someone lean over him with a knife and stab him to death without his even putting up any kind of defense?"

"Nobody expects to be stabbed to death by a friend they think is just playing," she said.

All three detectives tensed imperceptibly.

"You think a friend did it?"

She shrugged, gesturing slightly with her hands. "Don't you?"

Brody took the knife out of the drawer. She looked at it indifferently, as though she'd seen a lot of knives.

"Is this it?"

"It looks like it."

"Have you ever seen it before?"

"Not that I know of."

47

"You'd know of it if you'd seen it?"

"Everybody in Harlem carries a knife. Do you think I know everybody's knife by sight?"

"Everybody in Harlem don't carry this kind of knife," Brody said. "This is a hand-tooled, imported English knife with a blade of Sheffield steel. The only place we've found so far where it can be bought in New York City is at Abercrombie and Fitch's, downtown on Madison Avenue. It costs twenty bucks. Can you imagine a Harlem punk going downtown and paying twenty bucks for an imported hunter's knife, then leaving it sticking in his victim?"

Her face turned a strange shade of dirty yellow, and her dark brown eyes looked haunted.

"Why not? It's a free country," she whispered. "So they say."

"You're free to go now," Brody said.

No one moved as she got up and went across the floor, in the stiff, blind manner of a sleepwalker, and left the room.

Brody fumbled in his coat pockets for his pipe and plastic tobacco pouch. He took his time stuffing the battered brier pipe, then struck a kitchen match on the edge of the desk and got his pipe going.

"Who cut her throat?" he asked through a cloud of smoke, holding the pipe in his teeth.

Grave Digger and Coffin Ed avoided each other's gazes, and both appeared strangely embarrassed.

"Johnny," Grave Digger said finally.

Brody froze, but relaxed so quickly it was scarcely perceptible.

"Did she charge him?"

"No. It went as an accident."

The police reporter stopped fiddling with his notes and stared.

"How the hell can you get your throat cut accidentally?" Brody asked.

"She said he didn't intend to do it—that he was just playing."

"Playing kind of rough," the police reporter commented.

"Why?" Brody asked. "Why did he do it?"

"She hung on too long," Grave Digger said. "He wanted Dulcy and she wouldn't let go."

48

"And she still hangs on to him."

"Why not? He cut her throat, and now she's got him for life."

"It's a funny way to keep a man, is all I can say."

"Maybe. But don't forget this is Harlem. Folks here are happy just to be alive."

7

THEY CALLED CHINK next.

He said he'd started the night with a little friendly stud poker session in his room. It had broke up at one-thirty and he'd arrived at the wake at two A.M. He had left the wake at five minutes to four to keep a tête-à-tête with Doll Baby in her kitchenette apartment in the building next door.

"Did you look at your watch when you left?" Brody asked.

"No, when I went down in the elevator."

"Exactly where was Reverend Short when you left?"

"Reverend Short? Hell, I didn't pay no attention." He paused briefly, as though trying to remember, and said, "I think he was standing beside the coffin, but I can't be sure."

"What was happening outside when you got down to the street?"

"Nothing. A colored cop was standing there guarding the A&P store groceries on the sidewalk. He might remember seeing me."

"Was there anyone with him."

"No, not unless it was a ghost."

"All right, son, let's have the facts without the comedy," Brody said with irritation.

Chink said he'd waited for Doll Baby in the front hall and they had walked up to her apartment on the second-floor rear. But she hadn't been in the mood, so he'd gone out to pick up a few sticks of marijuana weed from a friend who lived down the street.

49

"Where?" Brody asked.

"Make a guess," Chink said defiantly.

Brody let it pass.

"Were there any people on the street that time?" he asked.

"Just as I stepped out on the sidewalk Dulcy Perry came from next door, and we saw Val's body in the bread basket at the same time."

"Had you noticed the bread basket before?"

"Sure. It was full of plain bread."

"There was no one else in sight when you and Dulcy met?"

"No one."

"How did she react when she saw her brother's body?"

"She just started going crazy."

"What did she say?"

"I don't remember."

Brody showed him the knife.

Chink admitted that it looked like the knife that had been stuck in Val's body, but denied ever having seen it before.

"Reverend Short testified that he saw you give this knife to Dulcy Perry in front of his church the day after Christmas, and that you showed her how to use it," Brody said.

Chink's sweaty yellow face paled to the color of a dirty sheet.

"That mother-raping preacher's blowing his top drinking that opium extract and cherry brandy," he raved. "I ain't given Dulcy any mother-raping knife and ain't never seen it before."

"But you've been after her like a dog after a bitch in heat," Brody charged. "Everybody says that."

"You can't hang a man for trying," Chink argued.

"No, but you can kill a woman's brother if he gets in the way," Brody said.

"Val wasn't no trouble," Chink muttered. "He'd have set it up for me if he hadn't been scared of Johnny."

Brody called in the harness cops.

"Hold him," he ordered.

"I want to call my lawyer," Chink demanded.

"Let him call his lawyer," Brody said. Then he asked if they'd picked up Doll Baby Grieves.

"Long time ago," one replied.

"Send her in."

Doll Baby had changed into a day dress that still looked like a nightgown in disguise. She sat on the stool in the circle of light and crossed her legs as though she liked being spotlighted in the same room with three men, even though they were cops.

She confirmed Chink's testimony, only she said he'd gone out for sandwiches instead of marijuana.

"Didn't you get enough to eat at the wake?" Brody asked.

"Well, we were just talking and that always makes me hungry," she said.

Brody asked about her relationship with Val, and she said they were engaged.

"And you were entertaining another man in your rooms at that hour of morning?"

"Well, after all, I had waited for Val 'til four o'clock, and I just figured he was out chasing." She giggled. "And what's good for the goose is good for the gander."

"He's dead now, or did you forget?" Brody reminded her.

She sobered suddenly and looked appropriately sad.

Brody asked her if she'd seen anyone when she left the wake. She said she'd seen a colored cop with the A&P store manager who'd just driven up. She recognized the manager because she shopped in the store, and she knew the cop personally. Both had greeted her.

"When did you last see Val?" Brody asked.

"He came to see me at about ten-thirty."

"Had he been to the wake?"

"No, he said he'd just come from home. I phoned Mr. Small and got the night off to attend Big Joe's wake—I generally work from eleven till four—and then me and Val sat there talking until one-thirty."

"Are you certain about the time?"

"Yeah, he looked at his watch and said it was one-thirty, and he'd have to leave in an hour because he wanted

51

to stop by Johnny's club before he went to the wake, and I said I wanted some fried chicken."

"You don't like Mamie Pullen's cooking," Brody suggested.

"Oh, sure, I like it fine, but I was hungry."

"You're a hungry girl."

She giggled. "Talking always makes me hungry."

"Where did you go for your fried chicken?"

"We got a taxi and went over to the College Inn at 151st Street and Broadway. We just stayed there for an hour, and then he looked at his watch and said it was two-thirty and he was going by Johnny's and would meet me at the Wake in about an hour. We got a taxi and he dropped me off at Mamie's and kept on downtown to Johnny's."

"What was his racket?" Brody shot at her.

"Racket? He didn't have any. He was a gentleman."

"Who were his enemies?"

"He didn't have any, unless it was Johnny."

"Why Johnny?"

"Johnny might have got tired of having him around all the time. Johnny's funny and awfully hot-headed."

"How about Chink? Didn't Val resent Chink's familiarity with his fiancée?"

"He didn't know about it."

Brody showed her the knife. She denied ever having seen it at any time.

He released her.

Dulcy was brought in next. She was accompanied by Johnny's attorney, Ben Williams.

Ben was a brown-skinned man of about forty, slightly on the fat side, with neatly barbered hair, and a heavy moustache. He was wearing the double-breasted gray flannel suit, horn-rimmed spectacles and conservative black shoes of the Harlem professional man.

Brody skipped the routine questions and asked Dulcy, "Were you the first one to discover the body?"

"You don't have to answer that," the attorney said quickly.

"Why the hell doesn't she?" Brody flared.

"The Fifth Amendment," the attorney stated.

"This isn't any Communist investigation," Brody said

disgustedly. "I can hold her as a material witness and let her talk to the Grand Jury, if that's what you want."

The attorney appeared to meditate. "Okay, you can answer," he said to Dulcy. After that he kept quiet; he had earned his money.

She said that Chink was standing beside the bread basket when she came out of the door.

"Are you certain of that?" Brody asked.

"I ain't blind," she retorted. "That's what made me look down to see what he was looking at, and then I saw Val."

Brody left it for a moment and started at the beginning of her career in Harlem. The gist of what he got had already been given.

"Did your husband give him an allowance?" Brody asked.

"Naw, he just slipped him money from his pocket whenever Val asked for a loan, and sometimes he'd let him win in the game. Then I gave him what I could."

"How long had he been engaged to Doll Baby?"

She laughed sarcastically. "Engaged! He was just keeping himself regular with that slut."

Brody dropped it and repeated the questions about Val's racket, enemies, whether he was carrying a large sum of money when he was killed, and asked her to describe the jewelry he was wearing. The wrist watch, gold ring and cuff links checked with what had been found on the body. She said the thirty-seven dollars found in his wallet would be about right.

Then Brody worked on the time element.

She said Val had left home about ten o'clock. He had said he was going to see a show at the Apollo Theatre—Billy Eckstein's band was doubling with the Nicholas brothers—and had asked to come with him, but she had an appointment with her hairdresser. So he'd decided to drop by the club and come with Johnny to the wake, and said they'd pick her up there.

She'd left home at twelve midnight with Alamena, who lived in a rented room downstairs in the same building.

"How long were you and Mamie locked in the bathroom?" Brody asked.

"Oh, a half hour, more or less. I can't be sure. When

I looked at my watch it was four-twenty-five, and Reverend Short began knocking on the door right then."

Brody showed her the knife and repeated what Reverend Short had said.

"Did Chink Charlie give you this knife?" he asked.

The attorney broke in to say she didn't have to answer that.

She began laughing hysterically, and it was five minutes before she had calmed down sufficiently to say, "He ought to get married, watching them Holy Rollers every Sunday and wanting to roll himself."

Brody turned red.

Grave Digger grunted. "I thought a Holy Roller preacher got the call to roll with all the sisters," he said.

"Most of 'em is," Dulcy said. "But Reverend Short's too full of visions to roll with anyone, unless it be a ghost."

"Well, that's all for now," Brody said. "I'm going to have you held in five-thousand-dollar bail."

"Don't worry about that," the attorney said to her.

"I ain't," she said.

Johnny was fifteen minutes late in appearing. His attorney had to telephone the bail-bondsman to arrange for Dulcy's bail, and he refused to be questioned without him.

Before Brody could fire his first question, the attorney produced affidavits given by Johnny's two helpers, Kid Nickels and Pony Boy, to the effect that Johnny had left his Tia Juana Club at the corner of 124th Street and Madison Avenue at 4:45 A.M., alone, and that Val had not been inside of the club all evening.

Without waiting to be questioned, Johnny volunteered the information that he hadn't seen Val since leaving his flat at nine the night before.

"How did you feel about supporting a brother-in-law who did nothing to deserve it?" Brody asked.

"It didn't bother me," Johnny said. "If I hadn't taken him in she'd have been slipping him money, and I didn't want to put her in the middle."

"You didn't resent it?" Brody persisted.

"It's just like I already said," Johnny stated in his toneless voice. "It didn't bother me. He wasn't a square, but he wasn't sharp, neither. He didn't have any racket, he

54

couldn't gamble, he couldn't even be a pimp. But I liked to have him around. He was funny, always ready for a gag."

Brody showed him the knife.

Johnny picked it up, opened and closed it, turned it over in his hand and put it back.

"You could turn a mother-raper every way but loose with that chiv," he said.

"You never saw it before?" Brody asked.

"If I had I'd have gotten me one like it," Johnny said.

Brody told him what Reverend Short had said about Chink Charlie giving Dulcy the knife.

When Brody had finished talking, there was no expression of any kind on Johnny's face.

"You know that preacher's off his nut," he said. His voice was toneless and indifferent.

They exchanged stares for a moment, both poker-faced and unmoving.

Then Brody said, "Okay, boy, you can go now."

"Fine," Johnny said, getting to his feet. "Just don't call me boy."

Brody reddened. "What the hell do you want me to call you—Mr. Perry?"

"Everybody else calls me Johnny—ain't that enough of a handle for you?" Johnny said.

Brody didn't answer.

Johnny left with his attorney at his heels.

Brody stood up and looked from Grave Digger to Coffin Ed. "Have we got any candidates?"

"You might try to find out who bought the knife," Grave Digger said.

"That was done the first thing this morning. Abercrombie and Fitch put six knives in stock a year ago, and so far they haven't sold any."

"Well, they're not the only store that sells hunting equipment in New York," Grave Digger argued.

"That won't get us nothing anyway," Coffin Ed said. "There's no way of telling who did it until we find out why it was done."

"That's going to be the lick that killed Nick," Grave Digger said. "That's the hard one."

"I don't agree," Brody said. "One thing is certain. He wasn't stabbed for money, so he must have been stabbed about a woman. *Churchy lay dame,* as the French say. But that don't mean another woman didn't do it."

Grave Digger took off his hat and rubbed his short kinky hair.

"This is Harlem," he said. "Ain't no other place like it in the world. You've got to start from scratch here, because these folks in Harlem do things for reasons nobody else in the world would think of. Listen, there were two hard working colored jokers, both with families, got to fighting in a bar over on Fifth Avenue near a hundred-eighteenth Street and cut each other to death about whether Paris was in France or France was in Paris."

"That ain't nothing," Brody laughed. "Two Irishmen over in Hell's Kitchen got to arguing and shot each other to death over whether the Irish were descended from the gods or the gods descended from the Irish."

8

ALAMENA WAS WAITING for them in the back seat of the car. Johnny and Dulcy got in the front, and the attorney got in the back beside Alamena.

A few doors down the street, Johnny pulled to the curb and turned about to bring both Dulcy and Alamena into vision.

"Listen, I want you women to keep buttoned up about this business. We're going to Fats's, and I don't want either one of you to start making waves. We don't know who did it."

"Chink did it," Dulcy said positively.

"You don't know that."

"The hell I don't."

He looked at her so long she began fidgeting.

"If you know it, then you know why."

56

She bit off a manicured nail and said with sullen defiance, "I don't know why."

"Did you see him do it?"

"No," she admitted.

"Then keep your goddam mouth shut and let the cops find out who did it," he said. "That's what they get paid for."

Dulcy began to cry. "You don't even care 'bout him being dead," she accused.

"I got my own ways about caring, and I don't want to see nobody framed if he didn't do it."

"You're always trying to play little Jesus Christ," Dulcy blubbered. "Why do all of us have to take the cop's gaff if I know Chink did it?"

"Because anybody might have done it. He's been asking for it all his mother-raping life. Him and you both."

No one said anything. Johnny kept looking at Dulcy. She bit off another manicured nail and looked away. The attorney squirmed about in his seat as if ants were stinging him. Alamena stared at Johnny's profile without expression.

Johnny turned about in his seat, eased the car from the curb and drove slowly off.

Fats's Down Home Restaurant had a narrow front, with a curtained plate-glass window beneath a neon sign depicting the outline of a man shaped like a bull hippopotamus.

Before the big Cad had pulled to a full stop, it was surrounded by skinny black children, clad in scant cotton clothes, crying, "Four Ace Johnny Perry . . . Fishtail Johnny Perry . . ."

They touched the sides of the car and the gleaming fishtails with bright-eyed awe, as though it were an altar.

Dulcy jumped out quickly, pushing the children aside, and hastened across the narrow sidewalk, her high heels tapping angrily, toward the curtained glass door.

Alamena and the attorney followed at a more leisurely pace, but neither bothered to smile at the children.

Johnny took his time, turned off the ignition and

57

pocketed the keys, watching the kids caress his car. His face was dead-pan, but his eyes were amused. He stepped out to the sidewalk, leaving the top down with the sun beating on the black leather upholstery, and was mobbed by the kids, who pulled at his clothes and stepped on his feet as he crossed the sidewalk toward the door.

He patted the Topsy-plaited heads of the skinny black girls, the burred heads of the skinny black boys. Just before entering he dug into his pockets and turned to scatter the contents of change over the street. He left the kids scrambling.

Inside it was cool, and so dark he had to take off his sun glasses on entering. The unforgettable scent of whisky, whores and perfume filled his nostrils, making him feel relaxed.

Wall light spilled soft stain over shelves of bottles and a small mahogany bar that was presided over by a giant black man in a white sport shirt. At sight of Johnny, he stood silently without moving, holding the glass he'd been polishing.

Three men and two women turned on their high bar stools to greet Johnny. Everything about them said gamblers and their women, whorehouse madams.

"Death always doubles off," one of the madams said sympathetically.

Johnny stood loosely, his big sloping-shouldered frame at perfect ease.

"We all gotta fall when we're on the turn," he said.

Their voices were low-pitched and without inflection, with the flat toneless quality of Johnny's. They talked in the casual manner of their trade.

"Too bad about Big Joe," one of the hustlers said. "I'm going to miss him."

"Big Joe was a real man," a madam said.

"You ain't just saying it," the others confirmed.

Johnny stuck his hand across the bar and shook the giant bartender's hand.

"What say, Pee Wee."

"Just standing here and moaning low, pops." He made a small gesture with the hand holding the half polished glass. "It's on the house."

"Bring us a pitcher of lemonade."

Johnny turned toward the arch leading toward the dining room at the rear.

"See you at the funeral, pops," a voice said behind him.

He didn't reply, because a man living up to his notices had stopped him with his belly. He resembled the balloon that had discovered stratosphere, but hundreds of degrees hotter. He wore an old-fashioned white silk shirt without the collar, fastened about the neck with a diamond-studded collar button, and black alpaca pants; but his legs were so large they seemed joined together, and his pants resembled a funnel-shaped skirt. His round brown head, which could have passed for a safety balloon in case his stomach burst, was clean-shaven. Not a hair showed above his chest—either on his face, nostrils, ears, eyebrows or eyelashes—giving the impression that his whole head had been scalded and scraped like the carcass of a pork.

"How's it going to chafe us, pops?" he asked, sticking out a huge, spongy hand. His voice was a wheezing whisper.

"Nobody knows 'til the deal goes down," Johnny said. "Everybody's just peeping at their hole cards now."

"The betting comes next." He looked down, but his felt-slippered feet, planted on the sawdust-covered floor, were hidden from his view by his belly. "I sure hate to see Big Joe go."

"Lost your best customer," Johnny said, rejecting the consolation.

"You know, Big Joe never ate nothing here. He just come in to gape at the chippies and beef about the cooking." Fats paused, then added, "But he was a man."

"Hurry up, Johnny, for God's sake," Dulcy called from across the room. "The funeral starts at two, and it's almost near one o'clock." She had kept on her sun glasses and looked strictly Hollywoodish in her pink silk dress.

The room was small, its eight square kitchen tables covered with white-and-red checked oilcloth planted in the inch of fresh, slightly damp sawdust covering the floor.

Dulcy sat at the table in the far corner, flanked by Alamena and the attorney.

"I'll let you go eat," Fats said. "You must be hungry."

"Ain't I always?"

The sawdust felt good beneath Johnny's rubber-soled shoes, and he thought fleetingly of how good life had been when he was a simple plough boy in Georgia, before he'd killed a man.

The cook stuck his head through the opening from the kitchen where the orders were filled and called, "Hiyuh, pops."

Johnny waved a hand.

Three other tables were occupied by men and women in the trade. It was strictly a hangout for the upper-class Harlem hustlers, those in the gambling and prostitution professions, and none others were allowed. Everybody knew everybody else, and all the diners greeted Johnny as he passed.

"Sad about Big Joe, pops."

"You can't stop the deal when the dealer falls."

Nobody mentioned Val. He'd been murdered, and nobody knew who did it. It was nobody's business but Johnny's, Dulcy's and the cops's; and everybody was letting it strictly alone.

When Johnny sat down the waitress came with the menu, and Pee Wee brought in a big glass pitcher of lemonade, with slices of lemons and limes and big chunks of ice floating about in it.

"I want a Singapore Sling," Dulcy said.

Johnny gave her a look.

"Well, brandy and soda then. You know good and well that ice-cold drinks give me indigestion."

"I'll have iced tea," the attorney said.

"You get that from the waitress," Pee Wee said.

"Gin and tonic for me," Alamena said.

The waitress came with the silver, glasses and napkins, and Alamena gave the attorney the menu.

He started to grin as he read the list of dinners:

Today's Special — Alligator tail & rice
Baked Ham — sweet potatoes & succotash

Chitterlings & collard greens & okra
Chicken and drop dumplings — with rice or sweet
potatoes
Barbecued ribs
Pig's feet à la mode
Neck bones and lye hominy

(*Choice of hot biscuits or corn bread*)

SIDE DISHES
Collard greens — okra — black-eyed peas & rice —
corn on the cob — succotash — sliced tomatoes and
cucumbers

DESSERTS
Homemade ice cream — deep-dish sweet potatoe pie —
peach cobbler — watermelon — blackberry pie

BEVERAGES
Iced tea — buttermilk — sassafras-root tea — coffee

But he looked up and saw the solemn expressions on the faces of the others and broke off.

"I haven't had breakfast as yet," he said, then to the waitress, "Can I have an order of brains and eggs, with biscuits?"

"Yes, sir."

"I want some fried oysters," Dulcy said.

"We ain't got no oysters. It ain't the month for 'em." She gave Dulcy a sly, sidewise look.

"Then I'll take the chicken and dumplings, but I don't want nothing but the legs," Dulcy said haughtily.

"Yes'm."

"Baked ham for me," Alamena said.

"Yes'm." She looked at Johnny with calf-eyed love. "The same as always, Mr. Johnny?"

He nodded. Johnny's breakfast, which never varied, consisted of a heaping plate of rice, four thick slices of fried salt pork, the fat poured over the rice, and a pitcher of blackstrap sorghum molasses to pour over that. With this came a plate of eight Southern-style biscuits an inch and a half thick.

61

He ate noisily without talk. Dulcy had drunk three brandy-and-sodas and said she wasn't hungry.

Johnny stopped eating long enough to say, "Eat anyway."

She picked at her food, watching the faces of the other diners, trying to catch snatches of their conversation.

Two people got up from a far table. The waitress went over to clear their places. Chink walked in with Doll Baby.

She had changed into a fresh pink linen backless dress, and wore huge black-tinted sun glasses with pink frames.

Dulcy stared at her with liquid venom. Johnny drank two glasses of ice-cold lemonade.

The room filled with silence.

Dulcy stood up suddenly.

"Where you going?" Johnny asked.

"I want to play a record," she said defiantly. "Do you have any objections?"

"Sit down," he said tonelessly. "And don't be so mother-raping cute."

She sat down and bit off another fingernail.

Alamena fingered her throat and looked down at her plate.

"Tell the waitress," she said. "She'll play it."

"I was going to play that platter of Jelly Roll Morton's, *I Want A Little Girl To Call My Own.*"

Johnny raised his face and looked at her. Rage started leaping in his eyes.

She picked up her drink to hide her face, but her hand trembled so she spilled some on her dress.

Across the room Doll Baby said in a loud voice, "After all, Val was my fiancé."

Dulcy stiffened with fury. "You're a lying bitch!" she yelled back.

Johnny gave her a dangerous look.

"And if the truth be known, he was just knifed to keep me from having him," Dolly Baby said.

"He'd already had a bellyful of you," Dulcy said.

Johnny slapped her out of her seat. She spun into the corner of the wall and crumpled to the floor.

Doll Baby let out a high shrill laugh.

Johnny spun his chair about on its hind legs.

"Keep the bitch quiet," he said.

Fats waddled over and put his bloated hand on Johnny's shoulder.

Pee Wee came from behind the bar and stood in the entrance.

Silently, Dulcy got back into her chair.

"Keep her quiet your God-damned self," Chink said.

Johnny stood up. Chairs scraped as everybody moved away from Chink's table. Doll Baby jumped up and ran into the kitchen. Pee Wee moved toward Johnny.

"Easy, pops," Pee Wee said.

Fats waddled quickly over to Chink's table and said, "Get her out. And don't you never come in here no more neither. Taking advantage of me like that."

Chink stood up, his yellow face flushed and swollen. Doll Baby came from the kitchen and joined him. As he left, walking high-shouldered and stiff-kneed, he said to Johnny, "I'll see you, big shot."

"See me now," Johnny said tonelessly, starting after him.

The scar on his forehead had swollen and come alive. Pee Wee blocked his path.

"That nigger ain't worth killing, pops."

Fats gave Chink a push in the back.

"Punk, you're lucky, lucky, lucky," he wheezed. "Git going before your luck runs out."

Johnny looked at his watch, giving Chink no more attention.

"We gotta go, the funeral's already started," he said.

"We all is coming," Fats said. "But you go on ahead 'cause you is the number two mourner."

9

HEAT SHIMMERED FROM the big black shiny Cadillac hearse parked before the door to the store-front church of the Holy Rollers at the corner of Eighth Avénue and 143rd Street. A skinny little black boy with big white shining eyes touched the red hot fender and snatched back his hand.

The black painted windows of what had been a super market before the Holly Rollers took it over reflected distorted images of the three black Cadillac limousines, and of the big flashy cars strung out behind the big cocky hearse like a line of laying hens.

People of many colors, clad in garb of all descriptions, their burr heads covered with straw hats of every shape, crowded about for a glimpse of the Harlem underworld celebrities attending Big Joe Pullen's funeral. Black ladies carried bright-colored parasols and wore green eyeshades to protect them from the sun.

These people ate cool slices of watermelon, spit out the black seeds and sweated in the vertical rays of the July sun. They drank quart bottles of beer and wine, and smaller bottles of pop and cola, from the flyspecked grocery stores nearby. They sucked chocolate-coated ice-cream bars from the refrigerated pushcart of the Good Humor man. They chewed succulent sections of barbecued pork-rib sandwiches, cast the polished bones to the friendly dogs and cats and the bread crusts to the flocks of molting Harlem sparrows.

Trash blew from the dirty street against their sweaty skin and into their gritty eyes.

The jumble of loud voices, strident laughter and the tinkle of the vendor's bells mingled with the sounds of mourning coming from the open church door and the loud summer thunder of automobiles passing in the street.

64

A picnic had never been better.

Sweating horse cops astride lathered horses, harness bulls with open collars and patrol cars with rolled-down windows rode herd.

When Johnny backed his big fishtail Cadillac into a reserved spot and climbed out behind Dulcy and Alamena, a murmur ran through the crowd and his name sprang from every lip.

Inside the church was like an airless oven. The crude wooden benches were jam-packed with friends who had come to bury Big Joe—gamblers, pimps, whores, chippies, madams, dining-car waiters and Holy Rollers—but were being cooked instead.

With his two women, Johnny pushed forward toward the mourners' bench. They found places beside Mamie Pullen, Baby Sis, and the pallbearers—who included a white dining-car steward; the Grand Wizard of Big Joe's lodge, dressed in the most impressive red-and-blue, gold-braided uniform ever seen on land or sea; a gray-haired, flat-footed waiter known as Uncle Gin; and two Holy Roller Deacons.

Big Joe's coffin, banked with hothouse roses and lilies of the valley, occupied the place of honor in front of the soapbox pulpit. Green flies buzzed above the coffin.

Behind it, Reverend Short was jumping up and down on the flimsy pulpit like some devil with the hotfoot dancing on red- and white-hot flames.

His bony face was quivering with religious fervor and streaming with rivers of sweat that overflowed his high celluloid collar and soaked into the jacket of his black woolen suit. His gold-rimmed spectacles were clouded. A band of sweat had formed about his trousers' belt and was coming through his coat.

"And the Lord said," he was screaming, swatting at the green flies trying to light on his face and spraying hot spit like a garden sprinkler. *"As many as I love, I rebuke and chasten. . . . Does you hear me?"*

"We hears you," the church members chanted in response.

"Be zealous therefore, and repent . . ."

". . . repent . . ."

65

"So I'm going to take my text from Genesis . . ."

". . . Genesis . . ."

"The Lord God made Adam in his image . . ."

". . . Lord made Adam . . ."

"Therefore I'm your preacher and I want to make a parable."

". . . preacher make parable . . ."

"There lies Big Joe Pullen in his coffin, as much of a man as Adam ever was, as dead a man as Adam ever will be, made in God's image . . ."

". . . Big Joe in God's image . . ."

"Adam bore two sons, Cain and Abel . . ."

". . . Cain and Abel . . ."

"And Cain rose up against his brother in the field, and he stuck a knife in Abel's heart and he murdered him . . ."

". . . Jesus Savior, murdered him . . ."

"I see Jesus Christ leaving heaven with all His grandeur, clothing himself in the garments of your preacher, making his face black, pointing the finger of accusation, and saying to you unrepented sinners, 'He who lives by the sword shall die by the sword . . .'"

". . . die by the sword, Lord, Lord . . ."

"I see Him point his finger and say, 'If Adam was alive today he'd be laying in that coffin dead and his name would be Big Joe Pullen . . .'"

". . . have mercy, Jesus . . ."

"And he'd have a son named Abel . . ."

". . . have a son, Abel . . ."

"And his son would have a wife . . ."

". . . son would have a wife . . ."

"And his wife would be the sister of Cain . . ."

". . . sister of Cain . . ."

"I can see Him step out on the rib bone of nothing . . ."

". . . rib bone of nothing . . ."

Spit drooled from the corners of his fishlike mouth as he pointed a trembling finger straight in Dulcy's direction.

"I can hear him say, 'Oh, you sister of Cain, why slayest thou thy brother?'"

A dead silence dropped like a pall over the cooking congregation. Every eye was turned on Dulcy. She cringed in her seat. Johnny stared at the preacher with a sudden

66

alertness, and the scar in his forehead came suddenly alive.

Mamie half arose and cried, "It ain't so! You know it ain't so!"

Then a sister in the amen corner jumped to her feet, with her arms stretched upward and her splayed fingers stiffened, and screamed, "Jesus in heaven, have mercy on the poor sinner."

Pandemonium broke loose as the Holy Rollers jumped to their feet and began having convulsions.

"Murderess!" Reverend Short screamed in a frenzy.

". . . murderess . . ." the church members responded.

"It ain't so!" Mamie shouted.

"Adulteress!" Reverend Short screamed.

". . . adulteress . . ." the congregation responded.

"You lying mother-raper!" Dulcy shouted, finally finding her voice.

"Let him rave on," Johnny said, his face wooden and his voice toneless.

"Fornication!" Reverend Short screamed.

At the mention of fornication the joint went mad.

Holy Rollers fell to the floor, frothing at the mouth, rolled and threshed, screaming, "Fornication . . . fornication . . ."

Men and women wrestled and rolled. Benches were splintered. The church rocked. The coffin shook. A big stink of sweating bodies arose. "Fornication . . . fornication . . ." the religious, mad people screamed.

"I'm getting out of here," Dulcy said, getting to her feet.

"Sit down," Johnny said. "These religious folks are dangerous."

The church organist began jamming the chorus of *Roberta Lee* on the church harmonium trying to restore order, and a big fat dining-car waiter cut loose in a high tenor voice:

> *"Dis world is high,*
> *Dis world is low,*
> *Dis world is deep and wide,*

67

> *But de longes' road I ever did see,*
> *Was de one I walked and cried . . ."*

Thoughts of the long road brought the fanatics to their feet. They brushed off their clothes and sheepishly straightened up the broken benches, and the organist went into *Roll, Jordan, Roll.*

But Reverend Short had gone beyond restraint. He'd left the pulpit and come down in front of the coffin to shake his finger in Dulcy's face. The undertaker's two assistants threw him to the floor and knelt on him until he'd calmed down; then the business of the funeral proceeded.

The congregation arose to the harmonium strains of *Nearer My God To Thee* and filed past the coffin for a last look at Big Joe Pullen's mortal remains. Those on the mourners' bench were the last to pass, and when the coffin lid was finally closed Mamie flung herself across it, crying, "Don't go, Joe, don't leave me here all alone."

The undertaker pried her loose, and Johnny put his arm about her waist and started guiding her toward the exit. But the undertaker stopped him, tugging at his sleeve.

"You're the chief pallbearer, Mr. Perry, you can't go."

Johnny turned Mamie over to the care of Dulcy and Alamena.

"Go along with her," he said.

Then he took his place with the five other pallbearers, and they lifted the coffin, bore it down the cleared aisle and between the lines of police on the sidewalk and slid it into the hearse.

Members of Big Joe's lodge were lined up in parade formation in the street, clad in their full regalia of scarlet coats with gold braid, light blue trousers with gold stripes, and headed by the lodge band.

The band broke out with *The Coming of John,* and the people in the street joined in singing with the choir.

The funeral procession, led by the hearse, fell in behind the marching lodge brothers.

Dulcy and Alamena sat flanking Mamie Pullen in the first of the black limousines.

Johnny rode alone behind the third limousine in his big open-top fishtail Cadillac.

Two cars behind him, Chink and Doll Baby followed in a blue Buick convertible.

The band was playing the old funeral chant in swingtime, and the trumpet player took a chorus and rode the staccato notes clear and high in the hot Harlem sky. The crowd was electrified. The people broke loose in mass hysteria, marching in swingtime. But they marched in all directions, forward, backward, circling, zigzagging, their bodies gyrating to the rocking syncopation. They went rocking and rolling back and forth across the street, between the parked cars, up and down the sidewalks, sometimes a boy taking a whirl with a girl, most times marching alone to the music, but not in time with the music. They were marching and dancing to the rhythm, between the beats, not on them, marching and dancing to the feeling of the swing, and still keeping up with the slowly moving procession.

The procession went down Eighth Avenue to 125th Street, east to Seventh Avenue, turned the corner by the Theresa Hotel and went north toward the 155th Street Bridge to the Bronx.

But at the bridge the band pulled up, the marchers halted, the crowd began to disperse, the procession thinned out. Harlem ended at the bridge, and only the principals crossed into the Bronx and made the long journey out Bronx Park Road, past the Bronx Park Zoo, to Woodlawn Cemetery.

The built-in record player in the hearse began playing an organ recording, the thin saccharine notes drifting back over the procession from the amplifiers.

They went through the arched gateway into the huge cemetery and stopped in a long line behind the yellow clay mouth of the open grave.

The mourners encircled the grave while the pallbearers lifted the coffin from the hearse and placed it upon a mechanical derrick that lowered it slowly into the grave.

An organ recording of *Swing Low, Sweet Chariot* began playing, and the choir sang a moaning accompaniment.

Reverend Short had gotten himself under control and stood at the head of the grave, intoning in his croaking voice:

"... in the sweat of thy face shalt thou eat bread, till thou return unto the ground; for out of it was thou taken: for dust thou art, and unto dust shalt thou return ..."

When the coffin touched the bottom of the grave, Mamie Pullen screamed and tried to throw herself after it. While Johnny was holding her, Dulcy suddenly crumpled and swayed toward the edge of the pit. Alamena clutched her about the waist, but Chink Charlie stepped forward from behind and put his arm about Dulcy and laid her upon the grass. Johnny caught a glimpse of them out of the corner of his eye, and he pushed Mamie into the arms of a deacon and wheeled toward Chink, his eyes yellow with rage and the scar on his forehead livid and crawling with a life of its own.

Chink saw him coming, stepped back and tried to pull his knife. Johnny feinted with his left and kicked Chink on the right shin. The sharp bone pain doubled Chink forward from the head down. Before the reflex motion had ceased, Johnny hit Chink back of the ear with a clubbing right; and when Chink fell reeling to his hands and knees, Johnny kicked at his head with his left foot, but missed it and grazed Chink's left shoulder instead. His lightning glance saw a spade in a grave digger's hand, and he snatched it out and swung the edge at the back of Chink's neck. Big Tiny from Fats's restaurant had closed in to stop Johnny and grabbed at his arm as he swung the spade. He didn't get a grip but managed to turn Johnny's arm so the flat of the spade instead of the edge hit Chink in the middle of the back and knocked him head over heels into the grave, on top of the coffin.

Then Tiny and half a dozen other men disarmed Johnny and wrestled him back to the gravel drive behind the plot of graves.

Johnny was circled in by his underworld friends, with Fats wheezing, "God damn it, Johnny, let's don't have no more killings. That wasn't nothing to get that mad about."

Johnny shook off their hands and straightened his dis-

70

arranged clothes. "I don't want that half-white mother-raper to touch her," he said in his toneless voice.

"Jesus Christ, she'd fainted," Fats wheezed.

"Not even if she's dropping stone-cold dead," Johnny said.

His friends shook their heads.

"You have hurt him enough for one day anyway, chief," Kid Nickels said.

"I ain't going to hurt him no more," Johnny said. "Just bring my womenfolks over to the car. I'm going to take them home."

He went over and got into his car.

A moment later the music ceased. The undertaker's equipment was removed from about the grave. The grave diggers began spading in the earth. The silent mourners slowly returned to the cars.

Mamie came between Dulcy and Alamena and got into the back of Johnny's car with Alamena. Baby Sis followed silently.

"Lord, Lord," Mamie said in a moaning voice. "They ain't nothing but trouble on this earth, but I know my time ain't long."

10

ON LEAVING THE cemetery, the procession disbanded and each car went its own way.

Just before turning into the bridge back to Harlem, Johnny got held up by a traffic jam caused by Yankee Stadium letting out after a ball game.

He and Dulcy, along with other well-heeled Harlem pimps, madams and numbers bankers, lived on the sixth floor of the flashy Roger Morris apartment house. It stood at the corner of 157th Street and Edgecombe Drive, on Coogan's Bluff, overlooking the Polo Grounds, the Harlem River and the inclined streets of the Bronx beyond.

71

It was seven o'clock when Johnny pulled his fishtail Cadillac before the entrance.

"I've come a long way from an Alabama cotton chopper to lose it all now," he said.

Everybody in the car looked at him, but only Dulcy spoke. "What you talking about?" she said warily.

He didn't answer.

Mamie's joints creaked as she started to alight.

"Come on, Baby Sis, we'll get a taxi," she said.

"You're coming up and eat with us," Johnny said. "Baby Sis and Alamena can fix supper."

She shook her head. "Me and Baby Sis will just go on home. I don't want to start being no trouble to nobody."

"It won't be no trouble," Johnny said.

"I ain't hungry," Mamie said. "I just want to go home and lie down and get some sleep. I'm powerfully tired."

"It ain't good for you to be alone now," Johnny argued. "Now's when you need to be around folks."

"Baby Sis'll be there, Johnny, and I just wanna sleep."

"Okay, I'll drive you home," Johnny said. "You know you ain't gotta ride in a taxi long as I got a car that'll run."

No one moved.

He turned to Dulcy and said, "You and Alamena get the hell out. I didn't say I was taking you."

"I'm getting good and tired of you hollering at me," Dulcy said angrily, getting from the car with a flounce. "I ain't no dog."

Johnny gave her a warning look but didn't answer.

Alamena got out of the back seat, and Mamie got in front with Johnny and put a hand over her closed eyes to shut out the terrible day.

They drove to her apartment without talking.

After Baby Sis had left them and gone inside, Mamie said, "Johnny, you're too hard on womenfolks. You expects them to act like men."

"I just expect them to do what they're told and what they're supposed to do."

She gave a long, sad sigh. "Most women does, Johnny, but they just got their own ways of doing it, and that's what you don't understand."

They were silent for a moment, watching the crowds on the sidewalk drift past in the twilight.

It was a street of paradox: unwed young mothers, suckling their infants, living on a prayer; fat black racketeers coasting past in big bright-colored convertibles with their solid gold babes, carrying huge sums of money on their person; hardworking men, holding up the buildings with their shoulders, talking in loud voices up there in Harlem where the white bosses couldn't hear them; teen-age gangsters grouping for a gang fight, smoking marijuana weed to get up their courage; everybody escaping the hotbox rooms they lived in, seeking respite in a street made hotter by the automobile exhaust and the heat released by the concrete walls and walks.

Finally Mamie said, "Don't kill him, Johnny. I'm an old lady and I tell you there ain't any reason."

Johnny kept looking at the stream of cars passing in the street. "Either's he's pressing her or she's asking for it. What do you want me to believe?"

"It ain't drawn that fine, Johnny. I'm an old lady, and I tell you, it ain't drawn that fine. You're splitting snake hairs. He's just a show-off and she just likes attention, that's all."

"He's gonna look good in a shroud," Johnny said.

"Take it from an old lady, Johnny," she said. "You don't give her no attention. You got your own affairs, your gambling club and everything, which takes up all your time, and she ain't got nothing."

"Aunt Mamie, that was the same trouble with my ma," he said. "Pete worked hard for her, but she wasn't satisfied 'less she was messing 'round with other men, and I had to kill him to keep him from killing her. But it was my ma who was wrong, and I always knowed it."

"I know, Johnny, but Dulcy ain't like that," Mamie argued. "She ain't messing around with nobody, but you gotta be patient with her. She's young. You knew how young she was when you married her."

"She ain't that young," he said in his toneless voice, still without looking at Mamie. "And if she ain't messing around with him then he's messing around with her—there ain't no two ways about it."

73

"Give her a chance, Johnny," Mamie pleaded. "Trust her."

"You don't know how much I wanna trust that gal," Johnny confessed. "But I ain't gonna let her nor him nor nobody else make a chump out of me. I ain't gonna fatten no frogs for snakes. And that's final."

"Oh Johnny," she begged, sobbing into her black-lace bordered handkerchief. "There's already been one killing too many. Don't kill nobody else."

For the first time Johnny turned and looked at her.

"What killing too many?"

"I know you couldn't help it that time 'bout your ma," she said. "But you ain't got to kill nobody else." She was trying to dissemble, but she talked too quickly and in too strained a voice.

"That ain't what you meant," Johnny said. "You meant about Val."

"That ain't what I said," she said.

"But that's what you meant."

"I wasn't thinking about him. Not in that way," she denied again. "I just don't want to see any more blood trouble, that's all."

"You don't have to pussyfoot about what you mean," he said in his toneless voice. "You can call his name. You can say he was stabbed to death, right over there on the sidewalk. It don't bother me. Just say what you mean."

"You know what I mean," she said stubbornly. "I mean just don't let her be the cause of no more killings, Johnny."

He tried to catch her eye, but she wouldn't meet his gaze. "You think I killed him," he said.

"I didn't say no such thing," she denied.

"But that's what you think."

"I ain't said nothing like that and you know it."

"I ain't talking about what you said. What I want to know is why you think I wanted to kill him."

"Oh Johnny, I don't think no such thing that you killed him," she said in a wailing voice.

"That ain't what I'm talking about, Aunt Mamie," he said. "I want to know what reason you think I'd have for killing him. Whether you think I killed him or not

74

don't bother me. I just want to know what reason you think I'd do it for."

She looked him straight in the eyes. "There ain't any reason for you to have killed him, Johnny," she said. "And that's the gospel truth."

"Then why'd you start off pleading for me to trust Dulcy so much and then the next thing you're figuring she's done give me reason enough to kill Val. That's what I want to know," he persisted. "What kind of reasoning is that?"

"Johnny, in this game of life, you got to give her as much as you ask to get from her," she said. "You can't win without risking."

"I know," he admitted. "That's a gambler's rule. But I got to put in eight hours every day in my club. It's as much for her as it is for me. But that means she's got all the chances in the world to play me for a sucker."

Mamie reached her gnarled old hand over and tried to take his hard long-fingered hand, but he drew it back.

"I ain't asking for mercy," he said harshly. "I don't want to hurt nobody, either. If she wants him, all I want her to do is walk out and go to him. I ain't gonna hurt her. If she don't want him, I ain't gonna have him pressing her. I don't mind losing. Every gambler got to lose sometime. But I ain't gonna be cheated."

"I know how you feel, Johnny," Mamie said. "But you got to learn to trust her. A jealous man can't win."

"A working man can't gamble and a jealous man can't win," said Johnny, quoting the old gambler's adage. After a moment he added, "If it's like you said, ain't nobody going to get hurt."

"I'm going up and get some sleep," she said, getting slowly to the sidewalk. Then she paused with her hand on the door and added, "Somebody's got to preach his funeral. Do you know any preacher who'd do it?"

"Get your own preacher," he said. "That's what he likes best, to preach somebody's funeral."

"You talk to him," she said.

"I don't want to talk to that man," he said. "Not after what he said today."

75

"You got to talk to him," she insisted. "Do it for Dulcy's sake."

He didn't say anything, and she didn't say any more. When she vanished within the entrance he started the motor and drove slowly through the idling traffic up to the store-front Church of the Holy Rollers on Eighth Avenue.

Reverend Short lived in a room at the back that had once been a storeroom. The street door was unlocked. Johnny entered without knocking and walked down the aisle between the broken benches. The door leading to Reverend Short's bedroom was cracked open a couple of inches. The plate glass windows at the front were painted black on the inside three-quarters high, but enough twilight filtered through the dingy glass overtop to glint on Reverend Short's spectacles as he peered through the narrow opening of the door.

The spectacles withdrew and the door closed as Johnny skirted the soapbox pulpit, and he heard the lock click shut as he approached.

He knocked and waited. Silence greeted him.

"It's Johnny Perry, Reverend; I want to talk to you," he said.

There was a rustling sound like rats scurrying about inside, and Reverend Short spoke abruptly in his croaking voice. "Don't think I haven't been expecting you."

"Good," Johnny said. "Then you know it's about the funeral."

"I know why you've come and I'm prepared for you," Reverend Short croaked.

Johnny had had a long hard day, and his nerves were on edge. He tried the door and found it locked.

"Open this door," he said roughly. "How the hell you expect to do business through a locked door?"

"Aha, do you think you're deceiving me," Reverend Short croaked.

Johnny rattled the door knob. "Listen, preacher," he said. "Mamie Pullen sent me and I'm going to pay you for it, so what the hell's the matter with you."

"You expect me to believe that a holy Christian like Mamie Pullen sent you to—" Reverend Short began croak-

76

ing when all of a sudden Johnny grabbed the knob in a fit of rage and started to break in the door.

As though reading his thoughts, Reverend Short warned in a thin dry voice as dangerous as the rattle of a rattlesnake, "Don't you break down that door!"

Johnny snatched his hand back as though a snake had struck at him. "What's wrong with you, preacher, you got a woman in there with you?" he asked suspiciously.

"So that's what you're after?" Reverend Short said. "You think that murderess is hiding in here."

"Jesus Christ, man, are you stone raving crazy?" Johnny said, losing control of his temper. "Just open this mother-raping door. I ain't got all night to stand out here and listen to that loony stuff."

"Drop that gun!" Reverend Short warned.

"I ain't got no gun, preacher—are you jagged?"

Johnny heard the click of some sort of weapon being cocked.

"I warn you! Drop that gun!" Reverend Short repeated.

"To hell with you," Johnny said disgustedly, and started to turn away.

But his sixth sense warned him of imminent danger, and he dropped flat to the floor just before a double blast from a twelve-gauge shotgun blew a hole the size of a dinner plate through the upper panel of the wooden door.

Johnny came up from the floor as though he were made of rubber. He hit the door with a driving shoulder-block that had so much force it broke the lock and flung the door back against the wall with a bang loud enough to be an echo to the shotgun blast.

Reverend Short dropped the gun and whipped a knife from his side pants-pocket, so quick the blade was open in his hand before the shotgun clattered on the floor.

Johnny was charging head first so fast he couldn't stop, so he stuck out his left hand and grabbed the wrist of Reverend Short's knife hand and butted him in the solar plexus. Reverend Short's glasses flew from his face like a bird taking wing, and he fell backwards across an unmade bed with a white-painted iron frame. Johnny landed on top of him, muscle-free as a cat landing on four feet, and in the

77

same instant twisted the knife from Reverend Short's grip with one hand and began throttling him with the other.

His knees were locked about Reverend Short's middle as he put the pressure on his throat. Reverend Short's near-sighted eyes began bulging like bananas being squeezed from their skins, and all they could see was the livid scar on Johnny's blood-purple forehead, puffing and wriggling like a maddened octopus.

But he showed no signs of fear.

Just short of breaking the skinny neck Johnny caught himself. He took a deep breath, and his whole body shuddered as though from an electric shock to his brain. Then he took his hands from Reverend Short's throat and straightened up, still straddling him, and looked down soberly at the blue-tinted face beneath him on the bed.

"Preacher," he said slowly. "You're going to make me kill you."

Reverend Short returned his stare as he gasped for breath. When finally he could speak, he said in a defiant voice, "Go ahead and kill me. But you can't save her. They're going to get her anyway."

Johnny backed from the bed and got to his feet, stepping on Reverend Short's spectacles. He kicked them angrily from underfoot and looked down at Reverend Short lying supine in the same position.

"Listen, I want to ask you just one question," he said in his toneless, gambler's voice. "Why would she want to kill her own brother?"

Reverend Short returned his look with malevolence.

"You know why," he said.

Johnny stood dead still, as though listening, looking down at him. Finally he said, "You've tried to kill me. I ain't going to do nothing about that. You've called her a murderess. I ain't going to do nothing about that, either. I don't think you're crazy, so we can rule that out. All I want to ask you is *why?*"

Reverend Short's near-sighted eyes filled with a look of malignant evil.

"There's only two of you who would have done it," he said in a thin dry voice no louder than a whisper. "That's you and her. And if you didn't do it, then she did. And if you don't know why, then ask her. And if you think you're going to save her by killing me, then go ahead and do it."

"I ain't got much of a hand," Johnny said. "But I'll call it."

He turned and picked his way through the church benches toward the door. Light from the street lamps came in through the unpainted upper rim of the dingy front windows, showing him the way.

11

It was eight o'clock, but still light.

"Let's go for a ride," Grave Digger said to Coffin Ed, "and look at some scenery. See the brown gals blooming in pink dresses, smell the perfume of poppies and marijuana."

"And listen to the stool pigeons sing," Coffin Ed supplied.

They were cruising south on Seventh Avenue in the small battered black sedan. Grave Digger eased the little car behind a big slow-moving trailer truck, and Coffin Ed kept his eyes skinned along the sidewalk.

A numbers writer standing in front of Madame Sweetie-pie's hairdressing parlor, flashing a handful of paper slips with the day's winning numbers, looked up and saw Coffin Ed's baleful eyes pinned on him and began eating the paper slips as though they were taffy candy.

Hidden behind the big truck trailer, they sneaked up on a group of weedheads standing in front of the bar at the corner of 126th Street. Eight young hoodlums dressed in tight black pants, fancy straw hats with mixed-colored bands, pointed shoes and loud-colored sport shirts, wearing smoked glasses, and looking like an assemblage of exotic grasshoppers, had already finished one stick and were passing around the second one when one of them ex-

79

claimed, "Split! Here comes King Kong and Frankenstein."

The boy smoking the stick swallowed it so fast the fire burnt his gullet and he doubled over, strangling.

The one called Gigolo said, "Play it cool! Play it cool! Just clean, that's all."

They threw their switchblade knives onto the sidewalk in front of the bar. Another boy palmed the two remaining sticks and stuck them quickly in his mouth, ready to eat them if the detectives stopped.

Grave Digger smiled grimly.

"I could hit that punk in his belly and make him vomit up enough evidence to give him a year in the cooler," he said.

"We'll teach him that trick some other time," Coffin Ed said.

Two of the boys were beating the strangling boy on the back, the others began talking with big gestures as though discussing a scientific treatise on prostitution. Gigolo stared at the detectives defiantly.

Gigolo was wearing a chocolate-colored straw hat with a wide yellow band polka-dotted with blue. When Coffin Ed fingered his right coat lapel with the first two fingers of his right hand, Gigolo pushed his straw hat back on his head and said, "Nuts to them mother-rapers, they ain't got nothing on us."

Grave Digger drove on slowly without stopping, and in the rear-view mirror he saw the punk take the wet marijuana sticks from his mouth and start blowing on them to dry them.

They kept on down to 119th Street, turned back to Eighth Avenue, went uptown again and parked before a dilapidated tenement house between 126th and 127th Streets. Old people were sitting on the sidewalk in kitchen chairs propped against the front of the building.

They climbed the dark steep stairs to the fourth floor. Grave Digger knocked on a door at the rear, three single raps spaced exactly ten seconds apart.

For the space of a full minute no sound was heard. There was no sound of locks being opened, but slowly the door swung inward five inches, held by two iron cables at top and bottom.

"It's us, Ma," Grave Digger said.

The ends of the cables were removed from the slots and the door opened all the way.

A thin old gray-haired woman with a wrinkled black face, who looked to be about ninety years old, wearing a floor length Mother Hubbard dress of faded black cotton, stood to one side and let them pass into the pitch-dark hallway and closed the door behind them.

They followed her without further comment down to the far end of the hall. She opened a door and sudden light spilled out, showing a snuff stick in the corner of her wrinkled mouth.

"There he," she said, and Coffin Ed followed Grave Digger into a small back bedroom and closed the door behind him.

Gigolo sat on the edge of the bed with his fancy hat pushed to the back of his head, biting his dirty nails to the quick. The pupils of his eyes were big black disks in his tight, sweaty brown face.

Coffin Ed sat facing him, straddling the single straight-backed wooden chair, and Grave Digger stood glaring down at him and said, "You've had a bang of heroin."

Gigolo shrugged. His skinny shoulders jerked beneath the canary-colored sport shirt.

"Don't get him excited," Coffin Ed warned, and then asked Gigolo in a confidential tone of voice, "Who made the sting last night, sport?"

Gigolo's body began jerking as though someone had slipped a hot poker down the seat of his pants.

"Poor Boy got new money," he said in a rapid blurred voice.

"Who kind of money?" Grave Digger asked.

"Hard money."

"No green money?"

"If he is, he ain't showed it."

"Where's he likely to be at this time?"

"Acey-Deucey's poolroom. He's a pool freak."

Grave Digger asked Coffin Ed, "Do you know him?"

"This town is full of Poor Boys," Coffin Ed said, turning back to the stool pigeon. "What's he look like?"

"Slim black boy. Plays it cool. Working stiff jive. Don't

never flash. Looks a little like Country Boy used to look 'fore they sent him to the pen."

"How does he dress?" Grave Digger asked.

"Like I just said. Wears old blue jeans, T-shirt, canvas sneakers, always looks raggedy as a bowl of yakamein."

"Has he got a partner?"

"Iron Jaw. You know Iron Jaw."

Grave Digger nodded.

"But he don't seem to be in on this sting. He ain't showed outside today," Gigolo added.

"Okay, sport," Coffin Ed said, standing up. "Lay off the heroin."

Gigolo's body began to jerk more violently. "What's a man going to do? You folks keeps me scared. If anybody finds out I'm stooling for you I be scared to shake my head." He was referring to a story they tell in Harlem about two jokers in a razor fight and one says, Man, you ain't cut me, and the other one says, if you don't believe I done cut you, just shake you head and it goin' to fall off.

"The heroin isn't going to keep your head on any better," Coffin Ed warned.

On the way out, he said to the old lady who'd let them in, "Cut down on Gigolo, Ma, he's getting so hopped he's going to blow his top one day."

"Lawd, I ain't no doctor," she complained. "I don't know how much they needs. I just sells it if they got the money to pay for it. You know, I don't use that junk myself."

"Well, cut down anyway," Grave Digger said harshly. "We're just letting you run because you keep our stool pigeons supplied."

"If it wasn't for these stool pigeons you'd be out of business," she argued. "The cops ain't goin' to never find out nothing if don't nobody tell 'em."

"Just put a little baking soda in that heroin, and don't give it to them straight," Grave Digger said. "We don't want these boys blind. And let us out this hole, we're in a hurry."

She shuffled down the black dark hall with hurt feelings and opened the three heavy locks on the front door without a sound.

"That old crone is getting on my nerves," Grave Digger said as they climbed into their car.

"What you need is a vacation," Coffin Ed said. "Or else a laxative."

Grave Digger chuckled.

They drove over to 137th Street and Lenox Avenue, on the other side from the Savoy Ballroom, climbed a narrow flight of stairs beside the Boll Weevil Bar to the Acey-Deucey poolroom on the second floor.

A small space at the front was closed off by a wooden counter for an office. A fat, bald-headed brown-skinned man, wearing a green eyeshade, a collarless silk shirt and a black vest adorned with a pennyweight gold chain, sat on a high stool behind the cash register on the counter and looked over the six pool tables arranged crosswise down the long, narrow room.

When Grave Digger and Coffin Ed appeared at the top of the stairs, he greeted in a low bass voice usually associated with undertakers. "Howdy do, gentlemen, how is the police business this fine summer day?"

"Booming, Acey," Coffin Ed said, his eyes roving over the lighted tables. "More folks getting robbed, slugged and stabbed to death in this hot weather than usual."

"It's the season of short tempers," Acey said.

"You ain't lying, son," Grave Digger said. "How's Deucey?"

"Resting as usual," Acey said. "Far as I heard."

Deucey was the man he had bought the business from, and he had been dead for twenty-one years.

Grave Digger had already spotted their man down at the fourth table and led the way down the cramped aisle. He took a seat at one end of the table and Coffin Ed took a seat at the other.

Poor Boy was playing a slick half-white pool shark straight pool, twenty-no-count, for fifty cents a point, and was already down forty dollars.

The balls had been racked for the start of a new game. It was Poor Boy's break and he was chalking his cue stick. He looked slantwise from one detective to the other

83

and chalked his stick for so long the shark said testily, "Go head and break, man, you got enough chalk on that mother-raping stick to make a fifteen-cushion billiard shot."

Poor Boy put his cue ball on the marker, worked his stick back and forth through the circle of his left index finger and scratched. He didn't tear the velvet, but he made a long white stripe. His cue ball trickled down the table and tapped the racked balls so lightly as to barely loosen them.

"That boy looks nervous," Coffin Ed said.

"He ain't been sleeping well," Grave Digger replied.

"I ain't nervous," the shark said.

He broke the balls and three dropped into pockets. Then he settled down and ran a hundred without stopping, going from the break seven times, and when he reached up with his cue stick and flipped the century marker against the other ninety-nine on the line overhead, all the other games had stopped and jokers were standing on the table edges to get a look.

"You ain't nervous yet," Coffin Ed corrected.

The shark looked at Coffin Ed defiantly and crowed, "I told you I wasn't nervous."

When the rack man put the paper sack holding the stakes on the table, Coffin Ed got down from his seat and picked it up.

"That's mine," the shark said.

Grave Digger moved in behind, putting both the shark and Poor Boy between himself and Coffin Ed.

"Don't start getting nervous now, son," he said. "We just want to look at your money."

"It ain't nothing but plain United States money," the shark argued. "Ain't you wise guys never seen no money?"

Coffin Ed upended the bag and dumped the contents onto the table. Dimes, quarters and half dollars spilled over the green velvet, along with a roll of greenbacks.

"You ain't been in Harlem long, son," he said to the shark.

"He ain't goin' to be here long either," Grave Digger said, reaching out to flip the roll of greenbacks apart from the silver money. "There's your roll, son," he said. "Take it and find yourself another town. You're too smart

84

for us country dicks in Harlem." When the shark opened his mouth to protest, he added roughly, "And don't say another God-damned word or I'll knock out your teeth."

The shark pocketed his roll and melted into the crowd. Poor Boy hadn't said a word.

Coffin Ed scooped up the change and put it back into the paper sack. Grave Digger touched the slim black boy on his T-shirted shoulder.

"Let's go, Poor Boy, we're going to take a ride."

Coffin Ed made an opening through the crowd. Silence followed them.

They put Poor Boy between them in the car and drove around the corner and parked.

"What would you rather have?" Grave Digger asked him. "A year in the Auburn state pen or thirty days in the city jail?"

Poor Boy looked at him slantwise through his long muddy eyes. "What you mean?" he asked in a husky Georgia voice.

"I mean you robbed that A and P store manager this morning."

"Naw suh, I ain't even seen no A and P store this morning. I made that money shining shoes down at the 125th Street Station."

Grave Digger hefted the sack of silver in his hand. "It's over a hundred dollars here," he said.

"I was lucky pitching halves and quarters," Poor Boy said. "You can ask anybody who was round there this morning."

"What I mean, son," Grave Digger explained, "is that when you steal over thirty-five dollars that makes it grand larceny, and that's a felony, and they give you one to five years in the state stir. But if you coöperate, the judge will let you take a plea to petty larceny and save the state the cost of a jury trial and appointing state lawyers, and you get off with thirty days in the workhouse. It depends on whether you want to coöperate."

"I ain't stole no money," Poor Boy said. "It's like what I done said, I made this money shining shoes and pitching halves."

"That's not what Patrolman Harris and that A and P

store manager are going to say when they see you in that line-up tomorrow morning," Grave Digger said.

Poor Boy thought that over. Sweat started beading on his forehead and in the circles underneath his eyes, and oily beads formed over the surface of his smooth flat nose.

"Coöperate how?" he said finally.

"Who was riding with Johnny Perry when he drove down Seventh Avenue early this morning, just a few minutes before you made your sting?" Grave Digger asked.

Poor Boy blew air from his nose as though he'd been holding his breath. "I ain't seen Johnny Perry's car," he said with relief.

Grave Digger reached down and turned on the ignition and started the motor.

Coffin Ed said, "Too bad, son, you ought to have better eyes. That's going to cost you eleven months."

"I swear to God I ain't seen Johnny's big Cad in near-most two days," Poor Boy said.

Grave Digger pulled out into the street and began driving toward the 126th Street precinct station.

"Y'all gotta believe me," Poor Boy said. "I ain't seen nobody on all of Seventh Avenue."

Coffin Ed looked at the people standing on the sidewalks and sitting on the stoops uninterestedly. Grave Digger concentrated on driving.

"There warn't a car moving on the avenue, I swear to God," Poor Boy whined. " 'Ceptin' that store manager when he drove up and that cop what's always there."

Grave Digger pulled to the curb and parked just before turning into 126th Street.

"Who was with you?" he asked.

"Nobody," Poor Boy said. "I swear to God."

"That's just too bad," Grave Digger said, reaching toward the ignition key.

"Listen," Poor Boy said. "Wait a minute. You say all I'm goin' to get is thirty days."

"That depends on how good your eyes were at four-thirty this morning, and how good your memory is now."

"I didn't see nothing," Poor Boy said. "And that's the God's truth. And after I grabbed that poke I was running so fast I didn't have time to see nothing. But Iron Jaw might of seen something. He was hiding in a doorway on 132nd Street."

"Where were you?"

"I was on 131st Street, and when the man drove up Iron Jaw was supposed to start yelling bloody murder and draw the cop. But he ain't let out a peep, and there I was, had already done sneaked up beside the car, and I just had to grab the poke and run."

"Where's Iron Jaw now?" Coffin Ed asked.

"I don't know. I ain't seen him all day."

"Where does he usually hang out?"

"At Acey-Deucey's like me most times, else downstairs in the Boll Weevil."

"Where does he live?"

"He got a room at the Lighthouse Hotel at 123rd and Third Avenue, and if'n he ain't there he might be at work. He pick chickens at Goldstein's Poultry Store on 116th Street and sometimes they stay open 'til twelve o'clock."

Grave Digger started the motor again and turned into 126th Street toward the precinct station.

When they drew up before the entrance, Poor Boy asked, "It's gonna be like you say, ain't it? If I cop a plea I don't get but thirty days?"

"That depends on how much your pal Iron Jaw saw," Grave Digger said.

12

"I DON'T LIKE these mother-raping mysteries," Johnny said.

His thick brown muscles knotted beneath his sweat-wet yellow crepe shirt as he banged the lemonade glass on the glass top of the cocktail table.

"And that's for sure," he added.

He sat leaning forward in the center of a long green plush davenport, his silk-stockinged, sweaty feet planted on the bright red carpet. The veins coming from his temples were swollen like exposed tree roots, and the scar on his forehead wriggled like a knot of live snakes. His dark brown lumpy face was taut and sweaty. His eyes were hot, vein-laced and smoldering.

"I done told you a dozen times or more I don't know why that nigger preacher's been telling all those lies about me," Dulcy said in a whining defensive voice.

Johnny looked at her dangerously and said, "Yeah, and I'm good and God-damned tired of hearing you tell me."

Her gaze touched fleetingly on his tight-drawn face and ran off to look for something more serene.

But there wasn't anything serene in that violently colored room. The overstuffed pea green furniture garnished with pieces of blonde wood fought it out with the bright red carpet, but the eyes that had to look at it were the losers.

It was a big front corner room with two windows on Edgecombe drive and one window on 159th Street.

"I'm just as tired of hearing you ask me all those goddam questions as you is tired of hearing me tell you I don't know the answers," she muttered.

The lemonade glass shattered in his hand. He threw the fragments across the floor and filled another one.

She sat on a yellow leather ottoman on the red carpet, facing the blond television-radio-record set that was placed in front of the closed-off fireplace beneath the mantlepiece.

"What the hell are you shivering for?" he asked.

"It's cold as hell in here," she complained.

She had shed down to her slip, and her legs and feet were bare. Her toenails were painted the same shade of crimson as her fingernails. Her smooth brown skin was sandy with goose pimples, but her upper lip was sweating, accentuating the downy black hairs of her faint moustache.

The big air conditioner unit in the side window behind her was going full blast, and a twelve-inch revolving fan beside it on the radiator cover sprayed her with cold air.

Johnny drank his glass of lemonade and put the glass

down carefully, like a man who prided himself on self-control under any circumstances.

"No wonder," he said. "Why don't you get up and put some clothes on?"

"For Christsake, it's too hot to wear clothes," she said.

Johnny poured and gulped another glass of lemonade to keep his brain from overheating.

"Listen, baby, I ain't being unreasonable," he said. "All I'm asking you is three simple things—"

"What's simple to you ain't simple to nobody else," she complained.

His hot glance struck her like a slap.

She said with quick apology, "I don't know why that preacher's got it in for me."

"Listen to me, baby," Johnny went on reasonably. "I just want to know why Mamie all of a sudden begins pleading your case when I ain't even suspected you of doing nothing. Is that unreasonable?"

"How the hell do I know what goes on in Aunt Mamie's head?" she flared.

Then, on seeing rage pass across his face like summer lightning, she gulped a big swallow of the brandy highball she was drinking and strangled.

Spookie, her black cocker spaniel bitch, who had been resting at her feet, jumped up and tried to climb into her lap.

"And quit drinking so God-damned much," Johnny said. "You don't know what you're saying when you're drunk."

She looked about guiltily for a place to put the glass, started to put it on the television set, caught his warning look, then put it on the floor beside her feet.

"And stop that damn dog from lapping you all the time," he said. "You think I want you always covered with dog spit?"

"Get down, Spookie," she said, pushing the dog from her lap.

The dog stuck his hind leg into the highball glass and turned it over.

Johnny looked at the stain spreading over the red carpet and his jaw muscles roped like ox tendons.

"Everybody knows I'm a reasonable man," he said. "All I'm asking you is three simple things. First, how come that preacher tells the police a story about Chink Charlie giving you that knife?"

"For God's sake, Johnny," she cried, and buried her face in her hands.

"Get me straight," he said. "I ain't said I believed that. But even if the mother-raper had it in for you—"

At that moment the commercial appeared on the television screen, and four cute blonde girls wearing sweaters and shorts began singing a commercial in a loud cheerful voice.

"Cut off that mother-raping noise," Johnny said.

Dulcy reached up quickly and toned down the voice, but the quartet of beautiful-legged pygmies continued to hop about in happy, zippy pantomine.

The veins started swelling in Johnny's forehead.

Suddenly the dog began to bark like a hound treeing a coon.

"Shut up, Spookie," Dulcy said quickly, but it was too late.

Johnny leaped up from his seat like a raving maniac, overturning the cocktail table and pitcher of lemonade, sprang across the floor and kicked the bitch in the ribs with his stockinged foot. The bitch sailed through the air and knocked over a red glass vase filled with imitation yellow roses sitting on a green lacquered end table. The vase shattered against the radiator, spilling paper yellow roses over the red carpet, and the bitch stuck its tail between its legs and ran yelping toward the kitchen.

The glass cover of the cocktail table had shattered against the overturned pitcher, and fragments of glass mingled with lumps of ice on the big wet splotch made by the spilt lemonade.

Johnny turned around, stepped over the debris and returned to his seat, like a man who prided himself on his self-control under all circumstances.

"Listen, baby," he said. "I'm a patient man. I'm the most reasonable man in the world. All I'm asking you is—"

"Three simple things," she muttered under her breath.

He took a long deep breath and ignored it.

90

"Listen, baby, all I want to know is how in the hell could that preacher make that up?"

"You always want to believe everybody but me," she said.

"And how come he keep on saying it was you who did it?" he kept on, ignoring her remark.

"God damn it, do you think I did it?" she flared.

"That ain't what's bothering me," he said, brushing that off. "What's bothering me is why in the hell *he* thinks you did it? What reason has he got to think you had for doing it?"

"You keep talking about mysteries," she said, showing signs of hysteria. "How come it was you didn't see Val all last night. He told me for sure he was going by the club and coming with you to the wake. He ain't had no reason to tell me he was if he wasn't. That's a mystery to me."

He looked at her long and thoughtfully. "If you keep popping off on that idea, that will get us all into trouble," he said.

"Then what you keep blowing off at me with all those crazy ideas you got about me, as if you think I kilt him," she said defiantly.

"It don't bother me who kilt him," he said. "He's dead and that's it. What bother me is all these mother-raping mysteries about you. You're alive and you're my woman, and I want to know why in the goddam hell all these people keep thinking things about you that I ain't never even thought of, and I'm your man."

Alamena came in from the hall and looked indifferently at the debris scattered about the room. She hadn't changed clothes but had put on a red plastic apron. The dog peeped out from behind her legs to see if the coast was clear, but decided that it wasn't.

"You all going to sit here and argue all night or do you want to come and get something to eat?" Alamena said indifferently, as though she didn't give a damn whether they ate or not.

For a moment both of them stared at her blankly, without replying. Then Johnny got to his feet.

Thinking Johnny didn't see her, with quick furtive motions Dulcy snatched up the glass the dog had stepped into and poured it half full of brandy from a bottle she had cached behind the television set.

Johnny was walking toward the hallway, but he turned suddenly without a break of motion and slapped the glass from her hand. Brandy splashed in her face as the glass sailed through the air and went spinning across the floor.

She hit him in the face with her balled right fist as fast as a cat catching fish. It was a solid pop with fury in it, and it knocked tears from his eyes.

He turned in blind rage and clutched her by the shoulders and shook her until her teeth rattled.

"Woman!" he said, and for the first time she heard his voice change tone. It was deep, throaty and came out of his guts, and it worked on her like a aphrodisiac. "Woman!"

She shuddered and went candy. Her eyes got limpid and her mouth suddenly wet, and her body just folded into his.

He went as soft as drugstore cotton and pulled her to his chest. He kissed her eyes, her nose and throat, and bent over and kissed her neck and the curve of her shoulder.

Alamena turned quickly and went back to the kitchen.

"Why don't you believe me," Dulcy said against his biceps.

"I'm trying to, baby," he said. "But you got to admit it's hard."

She dropped her arms to her sides and he took his arms from around her and put his hands in his pockets. They went down the hall to the kitchen.

The two bedrooms, separated by the bathroom, were on the left side of the hall which opened onto the outside corridor. The dining room and the kitchen were on the right side. There was a back door in the kitchen, and a small alcove opening to the service staircase at the end of the corridor.

The three of them sat on the plastic-covered, foam-rubber cushioned chairs about an enamel topped table covered with a red-and-white checked cloth and helped themselves from a steaming dish of boiled collard greens, okra, and pigs feet, a warmed-over bowl of black-eyed peas and a platter of cornbread.

There was half a bottle of bourbon whisky on the table, but the two women avoided it and Johnny asked, "Ain't there no lemonade left?"

Alamena got a gallon jar from the refrigerator and filled a glass pitcher without comment. They ate without talking.

Johnny doused his food with red-hot sauce from a bottle with a label depicting two bright red, long-horned devils dancing in knee-deep bright red flames, and ate two heaping platefuls, six pieces of cornbread, and drank a half pitcher of ice-cold lemonade.

"It's hot as hell in here," he complained and got up and switched on a ten-inch revolving fan attached to the wall; then he sat down again and began picking his teeth with a wooden toothpick selected from the glass of toothpicks that remained on the table with the salt, pepper and other condiments.

"That fan ain't goin' to help you none with all that red devil sauce you've eaten," Dulcy said. "Some day your guts are going to catch on fire, and you ain't goin' to be able to get enough lemonade down inside of you to put it out."

"Who's going to preach Val's funeral?" Alamena asked.

Johnny and Dulcy stared at her.

Then Johnny started again. "If I hadn't just felt that mother-raper lowering the boom on me I'd be lying there right now blown half in two," he said.

Alamena's eyes stretched. "You mean Reverend Short?" she asked. "He shoot at you?"

Johnny ignored her question and kept hammering at Dulcy. "That don't bother me so much as why," he said.

Dulcy continued to eat without replying. Johnny's veins began to swell again.

"Listen, girl," he said. "I'm telling you, all I want to know is why."

"Well, for Christsake," Dulcy flared. "If I'm going to take the blame for what that opium-drinking lunatic does, I just may as well quit living."

The doorbell rang. Spookie began to bark.

"Shut up, Spookie," Dulcy said.

Alamena got up and went to the door.

She came back and took her seat without saying anything.

Doll Baby stopped in the doorway and put one hand on her hip.

"Don't bother about me," she said. "I'm practically one of the family."

"You've got the nerve of a brass monkey," Dulcy cried, starting to her feet. "And I'm going to shut your mouth right now."

"No you ain't," Johnny said without moving. "Just set down and shut up."

Dulcy hesitated for a moment, as though to defy him, but decided against it and sat down. If looks could kill, Doll Baby would have dropped stone-dead.

Johnny turned his head slightly and said to Doll Baby, "What do you want, girlie?"

"I just want what's due me," Doll Baby said. "Me and Val was engaged, and I got a right to his inheritance."

Johnny stared at her. Both Dulcy and Alamena stared at her, too.

"Come again?" Johnny said. "I didn't get that."

She waved her left hand about, flashing a brilliant stone set in a gold-colored band.

"He gave me this diamond engagement ring if you want proof," she said.

Dulcy let loose with a shrill, scornful laugh. "If you got that from Val it ain't nothing but glass," she said.

"Shut up," Johnny said to her, then to Doll Baby he said, "I don't need no proof. I believe you. So what?"

"So I got a right as his fiancé to anything he left," she argued.

"He ain't left nothing but this world," Johnny said.

Doll Baby's stupid expression gave way to a frown. "He must have left some clothes," she said.

Dulcy started to laugh again, but a look from Johnny silenced her. Alamena dropped her head to hide a smile.

"What about his jewelry? His watch and rings and things," Doll Baby persisted.

"The police are the people for you to see," Johnny

94

said. "They got all his jewelry. Go tell them your story."

"I'm going to tell them my story, don't you worry," she said.

"I ain't worrying," Johnny said.

"What about that ten thousand dollars you were going to give him to open a liquor store?" Doll Baby said.

Johnny didn't move. His whole body became rigid, as though it were suddenly turned into bronze. He kept his unblinking gaze pinned on her so long she began to fidget.

Finally he said, "What about it?"

"Well, after all, I was his fiancée and he said you were going to put up ten grand for him to open that store, and I guess I got some kind of widow's rights," she said.

Dulcy and Alamena stared at her with a curious silence. Johnny's stare never left her face. She began to squirm beneath the concentrated scrutiny.

"When did he tell you that?" Johnny asked.

"The day after Big Joe died—day before yesterday, I guess it was," she said. "Him and me was planning on setting up housekeeping, and he said he was going to get ten grand from you for sure."

"Listen, girlie, you're sure about that?" Johnny asked. His voice hadn't changed, but he looked thoughtful and puzzled.

"As sure as I'm living," Doll Baby said. "I'd swear it on my mother's grave."

"And you believed it?" Johnny kept after her.

"Well, after all, why shouldn't I?" she countered. "He had Dulcy batting for him."

"You lying whore!" Dulcy cried, and was out of her chair and across the room and tangling with Doll Baby before Johnny could move.

He jumped up and pulled them apart, holding them by the backs of their necks.

"I'm going to get you for this," Doll Baby threatened Dulcy.

Dulcy spat in her face. Johnny hurled her across the kitchen with one hand. She snatched a razor-sharp kitchen knife from the sideboard drawer and charged back across the room. Johnny released Doll Baby and turned to meet

95

her, spearing her wrist with his left hand and twisting the knife from her grip.

"If you don't get her out of here I'm going to kill her," she raved.

Alamena got up calmly, went out into the hall and closed the front door. When she had returned and taken her seat, she said indifferently, "She's already gone. She must have been reading your mind."

Johnny resumed his seat. The cocker spaniel bitch came out from beneath the stove and began licking Dulcy's bare feet.

"Get away, Spookie," Dulcy said, and took her own seat again.

Johnny poured himself a glass of lemonade.

Dulcy poured a water glass half full of bourbon whisky and drank it down straight. Johnny watched her without speaking. He looked alert and wary, but puzzled. Dulcy choked and her eyes filled with tears. Alamena stared down at her dirty plate.

Johnny lifted the glass of lemonade, changed his mind and poured it back into the pitcher. He then poured the glass one-third full of whisky. But he didn't drink it. He just stared at it for a long time. No one said anything.

He stood up without drinking the whisky, and said, "Now I got another mother-raping mystery," and left the kitchen, walking silently on his stockinged feet.

13

IT WAS AFTER seven o'clock when Grave Digger and Coffin Ed parked in front of Goldstein's Poultry Store on 116th Street between Lexington and Third Avenues.

The name appeared in faded gilt letters above dingy plate glass windows, and a wooden sihouette of what passed for a chicken hung from an angle-bar over the entrance, the word *chickens* painted on it.

Chicken coops, most of which were empty, were stacked six and seven high on the sidewalk flanking the entrance, and were chained together. The chains were padlocked to heavy iron attachments fastened to the front of the store.

"Goldstein don't trust these folks with his chickens," Coffin Ed remarked as they alighted from the car.

"Can you blame him?" Grave Digger replied.

There were more stacks of coops inside the store containing more chickens.

Mr. and Mrs. Goldstein and several younger Goldsteins were bustling about, selling chickens on the feet to a number of late customers, mostly proprietors of chicken shacks, barbecue stands, nightclubs and after-hours joints.

Mr. Goldstein approached them, washing his hands with the foul-scented air. "What can I do for you gentlemen?" he asked. He had never run afoul of the law and didn't know any detectives by sight.

Grave Digger drew his gold-plated badge from his pocket and exhibited it in the palm of his hand.

"We're the men," he said.

Mr. Goldstein paled. "Are we breaking the law?"

"No, no, you're doing a public service," Grave Digger replied. "We're looking for a boy who works for you called Iron Jaw. His straight monicker is Ibsen. Don't ask us where he got it."

"Oh, Ibsen," Mr. Goldstein said with relief. "He's a picker. He's in the back." Then he began worrying again. "You're not going to arrest him now, are you? I've got many orders to fill."

"We just want to ask him a few questions," Grave Digger assured him.

But Mr. Goldstein wasn't assured. "Please, sirs, don't ask him too many questions," he entreated. "He can't think about but one thing at a time, and I think he's been drinking a little, too."

"We're going to try not to strain him," Coffin Ed said.

They went through the door into the back room.

A muscular, broad-shouldered young man, naked to the waist, with sweat streaming from his smooth, jet-black skin, stood over the picking table beside the scalding vat, his back to the door. His arms were working like the driv-

97

ing rod of a speeding locomotive, and wet feathers were raining into a bushel basket at his side.

He was singing to himself in a whisky-thick voice:

> *"Cap'n walkin' up an' down*
> *Buddy layin' there dead, Lord,*
> *On de burnin' ground,*
> *If I'da had my weight in line,*
> *I'da whup dat Cap'n till he went stone blind."*

Chickens were lined up on one side of the big table, lying quietly on their backs with their heads tucked beneath their wings and their feet stuck up. Each one had a tag tied to a leg.

A young man wearing glasses come from behind the wrapping table, glanced at Grave Digger and Coffin Ed without curiosity, and walked over behind the picker. He pointed at one of the live chickens on the far corner of the table, a big-legged Plymouth Rock pullet, minus a tag.

"What's that chicken doing there, Ibsen?" he asked in a suspicious voice.

The picker turned to look at him. In profile his jaw stuck out from his muscle-roped neck like a pressing iron, and his flat-nosed face and sloping forehead slanted back at a thirty-degree angle.

"Oh, that there chicken," he said. "Well, suh, that there chicken belongs to Missus Klein."

"Why ain't it got a tag on it then?"

"Well, suh, she don't know whether she gonna take it or not. She ain't come back for it yet."

"All right, then," the young man said peevishly. "Get on with your work. Just don't stand there—we got these orders to fill."

The picker turned and his arms began working like locomotive driving rods. He began again to sing to himself. He hadn't seen the two detectives standing just inside the doorway.

Grave Digger gestured toward the door with his head. Coffin Ed nodded. They slipped out silently.

Mr. Goldstein deserted a customer for a moment as

98

they passed through the front room. "I'm glad you didn't arrest Ibsen," he said, washing his hands with air. "He's a good worker and an honest man."

"Yeah, we noticed how much you trust him," Coffin Ed said.

They got in their car, drove two doors down the street, parked again and sat waiting.

"I'll bet a pint of rye he gets it," Grave Digger said.

"Hell, what kind of bet is that?" Coffin Ed replied. "That boy has stole so many chickens from those Goldsteins he's one quarter chicken himself. I'll bet he could steal a chicken out of the egg without cracking the shell."

"Anyway, we're going to soon see."

They almost missed him. The picker left by the back door and came out into the street from a narrow walk ahead of them.

He was wearing a big loose-fitting olive drab canvas army jacket with a ribbed cotton collar and a drawstring at the bottom, and his nappy head was covered with a GI fatigue cap worn backward, the visor hanging down the back of his neck. In that getup his iron jaw was more prominent. He looked as though he had tried to swallow the pressing iron and it had sunk between his bottom teeth underneath his tongue.

He went over to Lexington Avenue and started uptown, staggering slightly but careful not to bump into anyone, and whistling the rhythm of *Rock Around The Clock* in high, clear notes.

The detectives followed in their car. When he turned east on 119th Street, they pulled ahead of him, drew in to the curb and got out, blocking his path.

"What you got there, Iron Jaw?" Grave Digger asked.

Iron Jaw tried to get him into focus. His large muddy eyes slanted upward at the edges and had a tendency to look out from opposite corners. When finally they focused on Grave Digger's face they looked slightly crossed.

"Why don't you folks leave me alone," he protested in his whisky-thick voice, swaying slightly. "I ain't done nothing."

Coffin Ed reached out quickly and pulled his jacket zipper open almost to the bottom. Smooth black shiny skin

99

gleamed from a muscular hairless chest. But, down near the stomach, black and white feathers began.

The chicken lay cradled in the warm nest at the bottom of the jacket, its yellow legs crossed peacefully like a corpse in a casket, and its head tucked out of sight underneath its outer wing.

"What are you doing with that chicken then?" Coffin Ed asked. "Nursing it?"

Iron Jaw looked blank. "Chicken, suh. What chicken?"

"Don't give me that cornfed Southern bull," Coffin Ed warned him. "My name ain't Goldstein."

Grave Digger reached down with his index finger and lifted the chicken's head from beneath the wing.

"This chicken, son."

The chicken cocked its head and gave the two detectives a startled look from one of its beady eyes, then it turned its head completely about and looked at them from its other eye.

"Looks like my mother-in-law whenever I have to wake her up," Grave Digger said.

All of a sudden the chicken started squawking and flapping about, trying to get out of its nest.

"Sounds like her, too," Grave Digger added.

The chicken got a footing on Iron Jaw's belly and flew toward Grave Digger, flapping its wings and squawking furiously, as though it resented the remark.

Grave Digger speared at it with his left hand and caught hold of a wing.

Iron Jaw pivoted on the balls of his feet and took off, running down the center of the street. He was wearing dirty canvas rubber-soled sneakers, similar to those worn by Poor Boy, and he was running like a black streak of light.

Coffin Ed had his long barreled nickel-plated pistol in his hand before Iron Jaw had started to run, but he was laughing so hard he couldn't cry halt. When he finally got his voice he yelled, "Whoa, Billy-boy, or I'll blast you!" and fired three rapid shots into the sky.

Grave Digger was hampered by the chicken and was late with his pistol, which was identical with Coffin Ed's. Then he had to clip the chicken in the head to save it for

100

evidence. When he finally looked up he was just in time to see Coffin Ed shoot the fleeing Iron Jaw in the bottom of the right foot.

The .38 caliber slug caught in the rubber sole of Iron Jaw's canvas sneaker and ripped it from his foot. His foot sailed out from underneath him, and he slid along the pavement on his rump. His flesh hadn't been touched, but he thought he'd been shot.

"They kilt me!" he cried. "The police has shot me to death!"

People began to collect.

Coffin Ed came up, swinging his pistol at his side, and looked at Iron Jaw's foot.

"Get up," he said, yanking him to his feet. "You haven't been scratched."

Iron Jaw tested his foot on the pavement and found that it didn't hurt.

"I must be shot somewhere else," he argued.

"You're not shot anywhere," Coffin Ed said, taking him by the arm and steering him back to their car.

"Let's get away from here," he said to Grave Digger.

Grave Digger looked about at the curious people crowding about. "Right," he said.

They put Iron Jaw between them on the front seat and the dead chicken on the back seat and drove east on 119th Street to a deserted pier on the East River.

"We can get you thirty days in the cooler for chicken stealing or we can give you back your chicken and let you go home and fry it," Grave Digger began. "It just depends on you."

Iron Jaw looked slantwise from one detective to the other.

"I don't know what y'all means, boss," he said.

"Listen, son," Coffin Ed warned. "Cut out that uncle tomming. Save it for the white folks. It doesn't have any effect on us. We know you're ignorant, but you're not that stupid. So just talk straight. You understand?"

"Yassuh, boss."

Coffin Ed said, "Don't say I didn't warn you."

"Who was riding with Johnny Perry when he drove down 132nd Street this morning just before Poor Boy

101

robbed the A and P store manager?" Grave Digger asked.

Iron Jaw's eyes stretched. "I don't know what you all is talking about, boss. I was dead asleep in bed all morning 'til I went to work."

"Okay, son," Grave Digger said. "If that's your story that'll cost you thirty days."

"Boss, I swear to God—" Iron Jaw began, but Coffin Ed cut him off, "Listen, punk, we've already got Poor Boy tagged for the job and are holding him for the morning court. He said you were standing in a doorway on 132nd Street just off of the Avenue, so we know you were there. We know that Johnny Perry drove past on 132nd Street while you were standing there. We're not trying to stick you for the robbery. We've already got you on chicken stealing. All we want to know is who was riding with Johnny Perry."

Sweat glistened on Iron Jaw's sloping, flat-featured face. "Boss men, I don't want no trouble with that Johnny Perry. I'd just as leave take my thirty days."

"There's not going to be any trouble," Grave Digger assured him. "We're not after Johnny. We're after the man who was with him."

"He stuck Johnny up and got away with two grand," Grave Digger improvised, taking a shot in the dark.

Iron Jaw whistled. "I thought there was something funny," he admitted.

"Didn't you notice that the man had a gun stuck in Johnny's side when they drove past?" Grave Digger said.

"Naw suh, I didn't see the gun. They drove up and parked just 'fore the corner, and the top was up and I couldn't see no gun. But I thought there was something funny 'bout them stopping right there as if they didn't want nobody to see 'em."

Grave Digger and Coffin Ed exchanged looks across Iron Jaw's stupid expression.

"Well, that pins that down," Grave Digger said. "He and Val had parked on 132nd Street before Poor Boy robbed the A and P store manager." He addressed his next question to Iron Jaw. "Did they get out of the car together or did Val get out alone?"

102

"Boss, I ain't seen no more that what I just told you, I swear to God," Iron Jaw declared. "When Poor Boy cut out with that poke, with that cop and that white man chasing him, there was a man looking out a window, and when they turned the corner it seemed like he tried to look around the corner to see where they was going, and the next thing I seed he was falling through the air. So I just naturally took off up Seventh Avenue, 'cause I didn't want to be there when the cops got there and started asking a lot of questions."

"You didn't notice how badly he was hurt?" Grave Digger persisted.

"Naw suh, I just figured he was dead and gone to Jesus," Iron Jaw said. "And it warn't like as if I was a big shot like Johnny Perry. If the cops found me there they was just liable as not to claim I pushed him out the window."

"You make me sad, son," Grave Digger said seriously. "Cops are not that bad."

"We'd like to let you take your chicken and go home and have your pleasure," Coffin Ed said. "But Valentine Haines was stabbed to death this morning, and we've got to hold you as a material witness."

"Yassuh," Iron Jaw said stoically. "That's what I mean."

14

IT WAS TEN-FIFTEEN at night when Grave Digger and Coffin Ed finally got around to calling on Chink Charlie.

First they'd had a foot race with a young man peddling skinned cats for rabbits. An old lady customer had asked for the feet, had become suspicious and called the police when told that they were nub-legged rabbits.

Then they'd had to interview two matronly Southern schoolteachers, living in the Theresa Hotel and taking summer courses at New York University, who had given a man posing as the house detective their money to put in the hotel safe.

They parked in front of the bar at 146th Street and St. Nicholas Avenue.

Chink had a room with a window in the fourth-floor apartment on St. Nicholas Avenue. He had chosen the black and yellow decor himself and had furnished it in modernistic style. The carpet was black, the chairs yellow, the day bed had a yellow spread, the combination television-record player was black trimmed with yellow, the small table-model refrigerator was black on the outside and yellow on the inside, the curtains were black-and-yellow striped, and the dressing table and chest of drawers were black.

The record player was stacked with swing classics, and Cootie Williams was doing a trumpet solo in Duke Ellington's *Take The A Train*. A ten-inch revolving fan on the sill of the open window blew in exhaust fumes, dust, hot air and the sound of loud voices from the congregation of whores and drunks in front of the bar down below.

Chink was standing in the glow of the table lamp in front of the window. His sweat-slick oily yellow body was clad in blue nylon boxer-type shorts. The fringe of a large purple-red scar, left by an acid burn, showed on his left hip above his blue shorts.

Stripped to her black nylon brassiere, black sheer nylon panties and high-heeled red shoes, Doll Baby was practicing her chorus routine in the center of the floor. She had her back to the window and was watching her reflection in the dressing-table mirror. A tray of dirty dishes containing leftovers from the chili bean and stewed chitterling dinners they'd ordered from the bar restaurant rested on the table top, cutting her reflection in half just below the panties, as though she might have been served without legs along with the other delicacies. The outline of three heavy embossed scars running across her buttocks were visible beneath the sheer black panties.

Chink was looking at them absently as they jiggled in front of his vision.

"I don't get it," he was saying. "If Val really thought he

was going to get ten G's from Johnny and wasn't just bull-ing you—"

She flared up. "What the hell's got into you, nigger. You think I can't tell when a man's talking straight?"

She had told Chink about her interview with Johnny, and they were trying to think up some angle to put the squeeze on him.

"Sit down, can't you!" Chink shouted. "How the hell can I think—"

He broke off to stare at the door. Doll Baby stopped dancing in the middle of a step.

The door had opened quietly, and Grave Digger had come into the room. While they were staring, he went quickly across to the window and drew the shade. Coffin Ed stepped inside, closed the door behind him and leaned back against it. Both wore their hats pulled low over their eyes.

Grave Digger turned and sat on the edge of the window table beside the lamp.

"Well, go on, son," he said. "What's the only way to figure it?"

"What the hell do you mean by breaking into my room like this?" Chink said in a choking voice. His yellow face was diffused with rage.

The window curtain beating against the fan guard made so much noise Grave Digger reached over and turned the fan off.

"What was that, son?" he asked. "I didn't hear you."

"He's beefing because we didn't knock," Coffin Ed said.

Grave Digger spread his hands. "Your landlady said you had company, but we figured it was too hot for you to be engaged in anything embarrassing."

Chink's face began to swell. "Listen, you cops don't scare me," he raved. "When you cross that threshold without a warrant I consider it as breaking and entering like two burglars, and I can take my pistol and blow your brains out."

"That's not the right attitude for a man first on the scene of a murder," Grave Digger said, standing erect.

Coffin Ed crossed the floor, pulled open the top drawer,

105

dug beneath a stack of handkerchiefs and brought out a Smith & Wesson .38 caliber pistol.

"And I've got a permit for it," Chink shouted.

"Sure," Coffin Ed conceded. "Your white folks down at the club where you work as a whisky jerker got it for you."

"Yeah, and I'm going to have them take care of you two nigger cops," Chink threatened.

Coffin Ed dropped Chink's gun back into the drawer. "Listen, punk—" he began, but Grave Digger cut him off.

"After all, Ed, be easy on the boy. You can see these two yellow people are not Negroes like you and me."

But Coffin Ed was too angry to go for the joke. He kept on talking to Chink. "You're out on bail as a material witness. We can pull you in any time we wish. We're trying to give you a break, and all we get from you is a lot of cute crap. If you don't want to talk to us here we can take you down and talk to you in the Pigeon Nest."

"You mean if I object to your pushing me around in my own house you can take me down to the precinct station and push me around there," Chink said venomously. "That's how you got to look like Frankenstein's monster, pushing people around."

Coffin Ed's acid-burned face went hideous with rage. Before Chink had finished speaking he had taken two steps and knocked him spinning across the yellow-covered bed. He had his long barreled pistol in his hand and was moving in to pistol-whip Chink when Grave Digger grabbed him by the arms from behind.

"This is Digger," Grave Digger said in a quick pacifying voice. "This is Digger, Ed. Don't hurt the boy. Listen to Digger, Ed."

Slowly Coffin Ed's taut muscles relaxed, as the murderous rage drained out of him.

"He's a mouthy punk," Grave Digger went on. "But he's not worth killing."

Coffin Ed stuck his pistol back into the holster, turned and left the room without uttering a word, stood for a moment in the corridor and cried.

When he returned Chink was sitting on the edge of the bed, looking sullen and smoking a cigarette.

Grave Digger was saying, "If you're lying about the knife, son, we're going to crucify you."

Chink didn't reply.

Coffin Ed said thickly, "Answer."

Chink replied sullenly, "I don't know nothing about the knife."

Grave Digger didn't look at his partner, Coffin Ed. Doll Baby had backed over to the far corner of the bed and was sitting on its edge as though expecting it to explode underneath her any moment.

Coffin Ed asked her suddenly, "What racket were you and Val scheming?"

She jumped as if the bed had blown up as expected.

"Racket?" she repeated stupidly.

"You know what a racket is," Coffin Ed hammered. "As many rackets as you've been up with in your lifetime."

"Oh, you mean did he have a hype?" She swallowed. "Val didn't do nothing like that. He was a square—well, what I mean is he was straight."

"How did you two lovebirds expect to live? On your salary as a chorus girl or were you intending to do a little hustling on the side?"

She was too scared to act indignant, but she protested meekly. "Val was a gentleman. Johnny was going to stake him to ten grand to open a liquor store."

Chink turned his head about and gave her a look of pure venom. But the two detectives just stared at her, and suddenly became completely still.

"Did I say something?" she asked with a frightened look.

"No, you didn't," Grave Digger lied. "You told us that before." He flicked a glance at Coffin Ed.

Chink said quickly, "That's something she dreamed up."

Coffin Ed said flatly, "Shut up."

Grave Digger said casually, "What we're trying to find out is why. Johnny's too tight a gambler for a deal that tricky."

"After all, Val was Dulcy's brother," Doll Baby argued stupidly. "And what's tricky about opening a liquor store?"

"Well, first of all, Val couldn't get a license," Grave Digger explained. "He did a year in the Illinois state

107

reformatory, and New York state doesn't grant liquor store licenses to ex-cons. Johnny's an ex-con himself, so he couldn't get the license in his own name. That means they'd have to bring a third party as a front to get the license and operate the business in his name. The profits would be split too thin, and neither Johnny nor Val would have any legal way of collecting."

Doll Baby's eyes had stretched as big as saucers during this explanation. "Well, he swore to me that Dulcy was going to get the dough for him, and I know he wasn't lying," she said defensively. "I had him hooked."

For the next fifteen minutes the detectives questioned Chink and her about Val's and Dulcy's past life, but came up with nothing new. As they turned to leave, Grave Digger said, "Well, baby, we don't know what game you're playing, but if what you say is true, you've just about cleared Johnny of suspicion. Johnny's hot-headed enough to kill anybody in a rage, but Val was killed with cold-blooded premeditation. And, if he was trying to shake Johnny down for ten grand, that would be the same as if Johnny left his name on the murder. And Johnny ain't the boy for that."

"Well how about that!" Doll Baby protested. "I give you a reason for Johnny to have done it and you turn around and say that proves he didn't do it."

Grave Digger chuckled. "Just goes to show how stupid cops are."

They went out into the hall and closed the door behind them. Then, after talking briefly with the landlady, they went down the hall, left by the front door and closed that door behind them.

Neither Chink nor Doll Baby spoke until they heard the landlady locking and bolting the front door. But the detectives had merely stepped outside, then had turned quickly and reëntered the flat. By the time the landlady was bolting the front door they had stationed themselves in front of Chink's bedroom door and were listening through the thin wooden panel.

The first thing Chink said, jumping to his feet and turning on Doll Baby furiously, was, "Why in the God-damned hell did you tell 'em about the ten grand, you God-damned idiot?"

"Well for Christ's sake," Doll Baby protested loudly. "Do you think I wanted them think I was goin' to marry a mother-raping beggar?"

Chink grabbed her by the throat and yanked her from the bed. The detectives glanced at each other when they heard her body thud against the carpeted floor. Coffin Ed raised his eyebrows interrogatingly but Grave Digger shook his head. After a moment they heard Doll Baby saying in a choked voice, "What the hell you trying to kill me for, you mother-raper?"

Chink had released her and had gone to the refrigerator for a bottle of beer.

"You've let the mother-raper out the trap," he accused.

"Well, if he didn't kill him, who did?" she said. Then she caught the expression on his face and said, "Oh."

"Whoever killed him it don't make no difference now," he said. "What I want to know is what he had on Johnny?"

"Well, I've done told you all I know," she said.

"Listen, bitch, if you're holding out on me—" he began, but she cut him off with, "You're holding out on me more than I'm holding out on you. I ain't holding out nothing."

"If you think I'm holding out anything, you had better just think it and not say it," he threatened.

"I ain't going to say nothing about you," she promised, and then complained, "Why the hell do you and me have to argue? We ain't trying to find out who killed Val, is we? All we're trying to do is shake Johnny down for a stake." Her voice began getting confidential and loving. "I'm telling you, honey, all you've got to do is keep pressing him. I don't know what Val had on him, but if you keep pressing him he's got to give."

"I'm going to press him all right," Chink said. "I'm going to keep pressing him until I test his mother-raping nerve."

"Don't test it too hard," she warned. "Cause he's got it."

"That ugly mother-raper don't scare me," Chink said.

"Look what time it is!" Doll Baby exclaimed suddenly. "I gotta go. I'm goin' to be late as it is."

Grave Digger nodded toward the outside door, and he

and Coffin Ed tiptoed down the hall. The landlady let them out quietly.

As they were going down the stairs, Grave Digger chuckled. "The pot's beginning to boil," he said.

"All I hope is that we don't overcook it," Coffin Ed replied.

"We ought to hear from Chicago by tomorrow or the day after," Grave Digger remarked. "Find out what they've dug up."

"I just hope it ain't too late," Coffin Ed said.

"All that's missing is just one link," Grave Digger went on. "What it was that Val had on Johnny that was worth ten G's. If we had that we'd have it chained down."

"Yeah, but without it the dog's running loose," Coffin Ed replied.

"What you need is to get good and drunk one time," Grave Digger told his friend.

Coffin Ed rubbed the flat of his hand down his acid-burned face. "And that ain't no lie," he said in a muffled voice.

15

IT WAS 11:32 O'CLOCK when Johnny parked his fishtail Cadillac on Madison Avenue near the corner and walked down 124th Street to the private staircase that led to his club on the second floor.

The name *Tia Juana* was lettered on the upper panel of the black steel door.

He touched the buzzer to the right of the doorknob once lightly, and an eye appeared immediately in the peephole within the letter *u* in the word *Juana*. The door swung open into the kitchen of a three-room flat.

A mild-mannered, skinny, bald-headed, brown-skinned man wearing starched khaki pants and a faded purple polo shirt said, "Tough, Johnny, two deaths back to back."

"Yeah," Johnny said. "How's the game going, Nubby?"

Nubby fitted the cushioned stump of his left arm, which was cut off just above the wrist, into the cup of his right hand and said, "Steady. Kid Nickels is running it."

"Who's winning?"

"I ain't seen. I been taking bets on the harness races for tonight at Yonkers."

Johnny had bathed, shaved and changed into a light green silk suit and a rose crepe shirt.

The phone rang and Nubby reached for the receiver on the paybox on the wall, but Johnny said, "I'll take it."

Mamie Pullen was calling to ask how Dulcy was.

"She's knocked herself out," Johnny said. "I left Alamena with her."

"How are you, son?" Mamie asked.

"Still kicking," Johnny said. "You get your sleep and don't worry 'bout us."

When he hung up Nubby said, "You look beat, boss. Why don't you just take a look about and cut back to the nest. Us three oughta be able to run it for one night."

Johnny turned toward his office without replying. It was located in the outer of the two bedrooms situated to the left of the kitchen. It contained an old-fashioned roll top desk, a small round table, six chairs and a safe. The room across from it, equipped with a big deal table, was used as a spare gambling room.

Johnny hung up his green coat neatly on a hanger on the wall beside his desk, opened the safe and took out a sheaf of money tied with brown paper tape on which was written: $1,000.

Beyond the kitchen was a bathroom, and then the hallway ran into a large front room the width of the flat with a three-window bay overlooking Madison Avenue. The windows were closed and the curtains drawn.

Nine players sat about a large round-top table, padded with felt and covered with soiled tan canvas, in the center of the room. They were playing a card game called Georgia Skin.

Kid Nickels was shuffling a brand-new deck of cards. He was a short black burr-headed man with red eyes and

111

rough pockmarked skin, wearing a red silk shirt several shades brighter than Johnny's.

Johnny walked into the room, put the sheaf of money on the table and said, "I'll take over now, Kid."

Kid Nickels got up and gave him his seat.

Johnny patted the sheaf of bank notes. "Here's fresh money that ain't got nobody's brand."

"Let's hope I latch on to some of it," Bad Eye Lewis said.

Johnny shuffled the cards. Crying Shine, the first player to his right, cut them.

"Who wants to draw?" Johnny asked.

Three players drew cards from the deck, showed them to each other to avoid duplication and put them on the table face down.

Johnny bet them ten dollars each for drawing. They had to call or turn in their cards. They called.

In Georgia Skin the suits—spades, hearts, clubs and diamonds—have no rank. The cards are played by denomination. There are thirteen denominations in the deck, the ace through the king. Therefore thirteen cards may be played.

A player selects a card. When the next card for that denomination is dealt from the deck, the first card loses. Skin players say the card has fallen. It goes into the dead, and can't be played again that deal.

Therefore a player bets that his card does not fall before his opponents' cards fall. If a player selects a seven, and the cards of all other denominations in the deck have been dealt off twice before the second seven shows, that player wins all the bets he has made.

Johnny spun the top card face upward and it dropped in front of Doc, the player who sat across the table from him. It was an eight.

"My hatred," Bad Eye Lewis said.

"I ain't got no hatred unless it be death," Doc said. "Throw down, all you pikers."

The players carried their bets to him.

Johnny edged up the deck and fitted it into the deal box, which was open on one side with a thumb-hole for dealing.

He spun the three of spades from the deck for his own card.

Soft intense curses rose in the smoky light as the cards spun face upward from the box. Each time a card fell the bets were picked up by the winners and the loser played the next clean card dealt from the deck.

Johnny played the three throughout the deal without it falling. He placed twelve bets and made a hundred and thirty dollars on the deal.

Chink Charlie staggered into the room, waving a handful of money.

"Make way for a skinner from way back," he said in a whisky-thickened voice.

Johnny was sitting with his back to the door and didn't look around. He shuffled the deck, edged it and put it down.

"Cut 'em, K.C.," he said.

The other players had looked once at Chink. Now they looked once at Johnny. Then they stopped looking.

"I don't suppose I'm barred from this mother-raping game," Chink said.

"I ain't never barred a gambler with money," Johnny said in his toneless voice without looking about. "Pony, get up and give the gambler your seat."

Pony Boy got up and Chink flopped into his seat.

"I feel lucky tonight," Chink said, slapping the money on the table in front of him. "All I want to win is ten grand. How 'bout it, Johnny boy? You got ten grand to lose?"

Once again the players looked at Chink, then back to Johnny, then at nothing.

Johnny's face didn't flicker, his voice didn't change. "I don't play to lose, buddy boy, you'd better find out that. But you can gamble here in my club as long as you got money, and walk out of here with everything you've won. Now who wants to draw?" he asked.

No one moved to draw a card from the deck.

"You don't scare me," Chink said, and drew one from the bottom.

Johnny charged him a hundred dollars. When Chink covered it he had only nineteen dollars left.

Johnny turned off the queen.

Doc played it.

Chink bet him ten dollars.

The queen of hearts doubled off.

"Some black snake is sucking my rider's tongue," somebody said.

Chink picked up the twenty dollars.

Johnny put the deck in the deal box and turned himself the three of spades again.

"Lightning never strikes twice in the same place," Bad Eye Lewis said.

"Man, don't start talking about lightning striking," Crying Shine said. "You're sitting right in the middle of a thunder storm."

Johnny turned off the deuce of clubs for Doc, who had first choice for a clean card.

Doc looked at it with distaste. "I'd rather be bit in the ass by a boa constrictor than play a mother-raping black deuce," he said.

"You want to pass it?" Johnny asked.

"Hell," Doc said, "I ain't gambling my rathers. Throw back, yellow kid," he said to Chink.

"That'll cost you twenty bucks," Chink said.

"That don't hurt the money, son," Doc said, covering it.

Johnny carried fifteen dollars to Doc, and began turning off the cards. Players reached for them, and bets were made. No one spoke. The silence grew.

Johnny sput the cards in the tight white silence.

A card fell. Hands reached for bets.

Doc fell again and looked through the dead for a clean card, but there wasn't any.

Johnny spun the cards and the cards fell. Chink's card held up. Johnny and Chink raked in the bets.

"I'll bet you some more, gambler," Johnny said to Chink.

"Throw down," Chink said.

Johnny carried him another hundred dollars. Chink covered it and had money left.

Johnny spun another card, then another. The veins roped in his forehead and the tentacles of his scar began to

114

move. Blood left Chink's face until it looked like yellow wax.

"Some more," Johnny said.

"Throw down," Chink said. He was beginning to lose his voice.

They pressed their bet another twenty dollars.

Johnny eyed the money Chink had left. He pulled a card halfway out of the box and knocked it back.

"Some more, gambler," he said.

"Throw down," Chink whispered.

Johnny carried fifty dollars to Chink.

Chink covered twenty-nine and passed the rest back.

Johnny spun the card. The seven of diamonds flashed in the spill of light and fell on its face.

"Dead men falls on their face," Bad Eye Lewis said.

Blood rushed to Chink's face, and his jowls began to swell.

"That's you, ain't it?" Johnny said.

"How the hell you know it's me, lest you reading these cards," Chink said thickly.

"It's got to be you," Johnny said. "It's the only clean card left."

The blood left Chink's face again, and it turned ashy. Johnny reached over and turned up the card that lay in front of Chink. The seven of spades looked up.

Johnny raked in the stack of money.

"You shot me, didn't you," Chink accused. "You shot me. You saw the seven-spot on the turn when you pulled it halfway out the box."

"You ain't got but one more time to say that, gambler," Johnny said. "Then you goin' to have to prove it."

Chink didn't speak.

"If you bet fast you can't last," Doc said.

Chink got up without speaking and left the club.

Johnny began losing. He lost all his winnings and seven hundred dollars from the bank. Finally he stood up and said to Kid Nickels, "You take over, Kid."

He went back into his office, took a .38 Army Colt revolver from the safe and stuck it inside of his belt to the left of the buckle, put his green suit jacket over his rose crepe shirt. Before leaving the club he said to Nubby, "If

I don't come back, tell Kid to take the money home with him."

Pony Boy came back to the kitchen to see if Johnny needed him, but Johnny was gone.

"That Chink Charlie," he said. "Death ain't two feet off him."

16

ALAMENA ANSWERED THE DOOR BELL.

Chink said, "I want to talk to her."

She said, "You're stark raving crazy."

The black cocker spaniel bitch stood guard behind Alamena's legs and barked furiously.

"What are you barking at, Spookie?" Dulcy called in a thick voice from the kitchen.

Spookie kept on barking.

"Don't try to stop me, Alamena, I warn you," Chink said, trying to push past her. "I've got to talk to her."

Alamena planted herself firmly in the entrance and wouldn't let him by.

"Johnny's here, you fool!" she said.

"Naw, he ain't," Chink said. "I just left him at the club."

Alamena's eyes widened. "You went to Johnny's club?" she asked incredulously.

"Why not," he said unconcernedly. "I ain't scared of Johnny."

"Who the hell is that you're talkin' to, Meeny?" Dulcy called thickly.

"Nobody," Alamena said.

"It's me, Chink," he called.

"Oh, it's you," Dulcy called. "Well, come on in then, honey, or else go 'way. You're making Spookie nervous."

"Hell with Spookie," Chink said, pushing past Alamena and entering the kitchen.

116

Alamena closed the entrance door and followed him. "If Johnny comes back and finds you here, he'll kill you sure as hell," she warned.

"Hell with Johnny," Chink fumed. "I got enough on Johnny to send him to the electric chair."

"If you live that long," Alamena said.

Dulcy giggled. "Meeny's scared of Johnny," she said thickly.

Both Alamena and Chink stared at her.

She was sitting on one of the rubber-cushioned kitchen chairs with her bare feet propped on the table top. She was clad only in her slip, with nothing underneath.

"Cops," she said, coyly, catching Chink's look. "You're peeping."

"If you weren't drunk I'd give you something to giggle about," Alamena said grimly.

Dulcy took her feet down and tried to sit straight.

"You're just mad 'cause I got Johnny," she said slyly.

Alamena's face went blank and she looked away.

"Why don't you get out and let me talk to her," Chink said. "It's important."

Alamena sighed. "I'll go up front and watch out the window for Johnny's car."

Chink pulled up a chair and stood in front of Dulcy with his foot on the seat. He waited until he heard Alamena enter the front room, then suddenly went and closed the kitchen door, came back and took his stance.

"Listen to me, baby, and listen well," he said, bending over and trying to hold Dulcy's gaze. "You're either going to get me those ten G's you promised to Val or I'm going to lower the boom."

"Boom!" Dulcy said drunkenly. Chink gave a violent start. She giggled. "Thought you wasn't scared?" she said.

Chink's face became mottled with red. "Listen, I ain't playing, girl," he said dangerously.

She reached up as though she'd forgotten his presence and began to scratch her hair. Suddenly she looked up and caught him glaring at her. "It's just one of Spookie's fleas," she said. He began swelling about the jowls, but she didn't notice. "Spookie," she called. "Come here, darling, and sit on Mama's lap." The dog came over and began to lick

117

her bare legs, and she picked it up and held it in her lap. "It's just one of your little black fleas, ain't it, baby?" she said, bending over to let the dog lick her face.

Chink slapped the dog from her lap with such savage violence it crashed against the table leg and began running about the floor yelping and trying to get out.

"I want you to listen to me," Chink said, panting with rage.

Dulcy's face darkened with lightning-quick fury and she tried to stand up, but Chink put his hands on her shoulders and pinned her in the chair.

"Don't you hit my dog, you mother-raper!" she shouted. "I don't allow nobody to hit my dog but me. I'll kill you quicker for hitting my dog—"

Chink cut her off. "God damn it, I want you to listen."

Alamena entered the kitchen hurriedly, and when she saw Chink holding Dulcy pinned to her seat she said, "Let her alone, nigger. Can't you see she's drunk?"

He took away his hands but said furiously, "I want her to listen."

"Well, that's your problem," Alamena said. "You're a bar jockey. Get her sober."

"You want to get your throat cut again?" he said viciously.

She didn't let it touch her. "No damned nigger like you will ever do it. And I'm not going to watch out for more than fifteen minutes, so you'd better get your talking done in a hurry."

"You don't need to watch out for me at all," Chink said.

"I ain't doing it for you, nigger, you needn't worry 'bout that," Alamena said as she left the kitchen and went back to her post. "Come on, Spookie." The dog followed her.

Chink sat down and wiped the sweat from his face.

"Listen, baby, you're not that drunk," he said.

Dulcy giggled, but this time it sounded strained. "You're the one that's drunk if you think Johnny's going to give you ten grand," she said.

"He ain't the one who's going to give it to me," he said. "You're the one who's going to give it to me. You're going

118

to get it from him. And you want me to tell you why you're going to do this, baby?"

"No, I just want you to give me time to brush off some of these hundred-dollar bills you see growing on me," she said, sounding more and more sober.

"There's two reasons why you're going to do this," he said. "First, it was your knife that killed him. The same one I gave you for Christmas. And don't tell me you've lost it, because I know better. You wouldn't carry it around with you unless you intended using it, because you'd be too scared of Johnny seeing it."

"Oh no you don't, honey," she said. "You ain't going to make that stick. It was your knife. You're forgetting that you showed me both of them when you told me that man down at your club, Mr. Burns, had brought them back from London and said one was for you and one was for your girl friend in case you got too handy with yours. I've still got the one you gave me."

"Let's see it."

"Let me see yours."

"You know damn well I don't carry that big knife around with me."

"Since when?"

"I ain't never carried it on me. It's at the club."

"That's just fine. Mine's at the seashore."

"I ain't joking with you, girl."

"If you think I'm joking with you, just try me. I can put my hand on my knife this minute. And if you keep pressing me about it I'm liable to get it and stick it into you." She didn't sound the least bit drunk any more.

Chink scowled at her. "Don't threaten me," he said.

"Don't you threaten me then."

"If you've still got yours, why didn't you tell the cops about mine?" he said.

"And have Johnny take the one I got and cut your throat and maybe mine too?" she said.

"If you're all that scared, why didn't you get rid of it?" he said. "If you think Johnny's going to find it and start chivving on you."

"And take a chance on you turning rat and saying it was

119

my knife that killed him?" she said. "Oh no, honey, I ain't going to leave myself open for that."

His face began to swell, but he managed to keep his temper.

"All right then, let's say it wasn't your knife," he said. "I know it was but let's just say it wasn't—"

"All together now," she cut in. "Let's say bull."

"All right then, let's say it wasn't your knife," he said. to shake Johnny down for ten grand. I know that for sure."

"And what I know for sure is that you and me ain't been drinking out the same bottle," she said. "You must have been drinking extract of gold or U.S. mint juleps, the way you keep talking about ten grand."

"You'd better listen to me, girl," he said.

"Don't think I ain't listening," she said. "I just keep hearing stuff that don't make any sense."

"I ain't saying it was your idea," he said. "But you were going to do it. That's for sure. And that means just one thing. You and Val had something on Johnny that was worth that much money or you'd never have gotten up the nerve to try it."

Dulcy laughed theatrically, but it didn't come off. "You remind me of that old gag where the man says to his girl, 'now let's both get on top.' That I'd like to see—just what me and Val had on Johnny that was worth ten grand."

"Well, baby, I'm going to tell you,' he said. "It ain't as if I need to know what you had on him. I know you had something on him, and that's enough. When that's tied together with the knife, which you claim you've still got but ain't showing nobody, that means a murder rap for one of you. I don't know which one and I don't care. If it don't hurt you, don't holler. I'm giving you your chance. If you pass, I'm going to Johnny. If he plays tough I'm going to have a little talk with those two Harlem sheriffs, Grave Digger and Coffin Ed. And you know what that's going to mean. Johnny might be tough, but he ain't that tough."

Dulcy got up and staggered over to the sideboard and drank two fingers of brandy straight. She tried to stand, but she found herself teetering and flopped into another chair.

"Listen, Chink, Johnny's got enough trouble as it is," she said. "If you press him just a little bit now, he'll blow his top and kill you if they burn him in hell for it."

He tried to look unimpressed. "Johnny's got sense, baby. He might have a silver plate in his head but he don't want to burn any more than anybody else."

"Anyway, Johnny don't have that kind of money," she said. "You niggers in Harlem think Johnny's got a back-yard full of money trees. He ain't no numbers man. All he's got is that little skin game."

"It ain't so little," Chink said. "And if he ain't got that kind of money, let him borrow it. He's got that much credit with the syndicate. And whatever he's got ain't going to do neither one of you no good if I drop the boom."

She sagged. "All right. Give me two days."

"If you can get it in two days you can get it by tomorrow," he said.

"All right, tomorrow," she conceded.

"Give me half now," he said.

"You know damn well Johnny don't have no five G's in this house," she said.

He kept pressing her. "How about you? Ain't you stole that much yet?"

She looked at him with steady scorn. "If you wasn't such a goddam nigger I'd stick you in the heart for that," she said. "But you ain't worth it."

"Don't try to kid me, baby," he kept on. "You got some dough stashed. You ain't the kind of chick to take a chance on getting kicked out on your bare ass."

She started to argue but changed her mind. "I've got about seven hundred dollars," she admitted.

"Okay, I'll take that," he said.

She got up and staggered toward the door. He stood up too, but she said, "Don't follow me, nigger."

He started to ignore her but changed his mind and sat down again.

Alamena heard her leave the kitchen and started back from the front room, but she called, "Don't bother, Meeny."

After a moment she returned to the kitchen with a

121

handful of greenbacks. She drew them across the table and said, "There, nigger, that's all I've got."

He started to get up and pocket the money, but the sight of the green patch on the red-and-white checked cloth nauseated her, and before he could reach the money she had bent over and vomited all over it.

He grabbed her by the arms and slammed her into a chair, cursing a blue streak. Then he took the filthy money to the sink and began washing it.

Suddenly the dog came tearing into the kitchen and began barking furiously at the door that led to the service entrance, which was in the corner of the kitchen. It opened into a small alcove which led into the service stairway. The dog had heard the sound of a key being inserted quietly in the lock.

Alamena came running into the kitchen on its heels. Her brown face had turned pasty gray.

"Johnny," she whispered, pressing her finger to her lips.

Chink turned a strange shade of yellow, like a person who'd been sick for a long time with yellow jaundice. He tried to ram the half washed, dripping wet money into his side coat-pocket, but his hands were trembling so violently he could scarcely find it. Then he looked wildly about as though he might jump out of the window if he weren't restrained.

Dulcy began laughing hysterically. "Who ain't scared of who?" she choked.

Alamena gave her a furiously frightened look, took Chink by the hand and led him toward the front door.

"For God's sake, shut up," she whispered toward Dulcy.

The dog kept barking furiously.

Then suddenly the sound of voices came from the back stairway.

Grave Digger and Coffin Ed had converged from the shadows the instant Johnny put his key in the lock.

In the kitchen they heard Grave Digger saying, "Just one minute, Johnny. We'd like to ask you and the missus some questions."

"You don't have to shout at me," Johnny said. "I ain't deaf."

"Occupational traits," Grave Digger said. "Cops talk louder than gamblers."

"Yeah. You got a warrant?" Johnny said.

"What for? We just want to ask you some friendly questions," Grave Digger said.

"My woman's drunk and ain't able to answer any questions, friendly or not," Johnny said. "And I ain't going to."

"You're getting kind of big for your britches, ain't you, Johnny," Coffin Ed said.

"Listen," Johnny said. "I ain't trying to be no big shot or play tough. I'm just tired. A lot of folks are pressing me. I pay a lawyer to talk for me in court. If you got a warrant for me or Dulcy, then take us. If you ain't, then let us be."

"Okay, Johnny," Coffin Ed said. "It's been a long day for everybody."

"Are you wearing your rod?" Grave Digger asked.

"Yeah. You want to see my license?" Johnny said.

"No, I know you got a license for it. I just want to tell you to take it easy, son," Grave Digger said.

"Yeah," Johnny said.

While they were talking, Alamena had let Chink out of the front door.

Chink had buzzed for the elevator and was waiting for it to come when Johnny let himself into the kitchen of his flat.

Alamena was washing the tablecloth. The dog was barking. Dulcy was still laughing hysterically.

"Why, imagine seeing you, daddy," Dulcy said in a blurred drunken voice. "I thought you were the garbage man, coming in that way."

"She's drunk," Alamena said quickly.

"Why didn't you put her to bed?" Johnny said.

"She didn't want to go to bed."

"Nobody puts Dulcy to bed when she don't want to go to bed," Dulcy said drunkenly.

The dog kept barking.

"She was sick on the tablecloth," Alamena said.

"Go home," Johnny said. "And take this little yapping dog with you."

"Come on, Spookie," Alamena said.

123

Johnny picked up Dulcy in his arms and carried her into the bedroom.

Outside in the corridor, Grave Digger and Coffin Ed joined Chink at the elevator doors.

"You're trembling," Grave Digger observed.

"Sweating, too," Coffin Ed added.

"I just got a chill is all," Chink said.

"Damn right," Grave Digger said. "That's the way to get chilled permanently, fooling around with another man's wife, and in his own house, too."

"I just been tending to my own business," Chink said argumentatively. "Why don't you cops try that sometime?"

"That's the thanks we get for giving you a break," Grave Digger said. "We held him up until you had time to get away."

"Don't talk to that son of a bitch," Coffin Ed said harshly. "If he says another word I'll knock out his teeth."

"Not before he talks," Grave Digger warned. "He's going to need his teeth to make himself understood."

The automatic elevator stopped on the floor. The three of them got in it.

"What is this, a pinch?" Chink asked.

Coffin Ed hit him in the solar plexus. Grave Digger had to restrain him. Chink walked out of the house between the two detectives, holding his stomach as though to keep it from falling out.

17

CHINK SAT ON the stool within the glaring circle of light in the Pigeon Nest, where Detective Sergeant Brody from Central Homicide had questioned him that morning.

But now he was being questioned by the Harlem precinct detectives, Grave Digger Jones and Coffin Ed Johnson, and it wasn't the same.

Sweat was streaming down his waxen face, and his beige

summer suit was wringing wet. He was trembling again and he was scared. He looked at the wet money stacked on one end of the desk through sick, vein-laced eyes.

"I've got a right to have my lawyer," he said.

Grave Digger sat on the edge of the desk in front of him, and Coffin Ed stood in the shadows behind him.

Grave Digger looked at his watch and said, "It's five minutes after two o'clock, and we've got to have some answers."

"But I've got a right to have my lawyer," Chink said in a pleading tone. "Sergeant Brody said this morning I had a right to have my lawyer when I was questioned."

"Listen, boy," Coffin Ed said. "Brody is a homicide man and solving murders is his business. He goes at it in a routine way like the law prescribes, and if some more people get killed while he's going about it, that's just too bad for the victims. But me and Digger are two country Harlem dicks who live in this village and don't like to see anybody get killed. It might be a friend of ours. So we're trying to head off another killing."

"And there ain't much time," Grave Digger added.

Chink mopped his face with a wet handkerchief. "If you think anybody's going to kill me—" he began, but Coffin Ed cut him off.

"I personally wouldn't give a goddam if you were killed—"

"Take it easy, Ed," Grave Digger said, and then to Chink, "We want to ask you one question. And we want a true answer. Did you give Dulcy the knife that killed Val as Reverend Short said you did?"

Chink squeezed out a laugh. "I've already told you, I don't know anything about that knife."

"Because if you did give the knife to her," Grave Digger went on talking softly, "and Johnny got hold of it and killed Val with it, he's going to kill her, too, if we don't stop him. That's for sure. And maybe if we don't get him soon enough he's going to kill you, too."

"You cops act as if Johnny was a black Dillinger or Al Capone—" Chink was saying, but his teeth were chattering so loudly he sounded as though he were speaking pig latin.

Grave Digger cut him off, still talking in a soft, persuasive voice. "And we know that you've got something on Dulcy, or else she wouldn't have let you in Johnny's house and taken the risk of talking to you for thirty-three minutes by the clock. And if it wasn't something goddam serious she wouldn't have given you seven hundred and thirty bucks to keep quiet." He banged the meaty edge of his fist on the stack of squashy money, jerked it back and wiped his hand with his handkerchief. "Dirty money. Which one of you puked on it?"

Chink tried to meet his gaze defiantly but couldn't do it, and his own gaze kept dropping until it rested on Grave Digger's big flat feet.

"So there are only two possibilities," Grave Digger went on. "You either gave her the knife or else you found out what Val knew about her that he was going to use to make her dig ten grand out of Johnny. And we don't figure you found that out since we talked to you because we've been shadowing you, and we know you went straight from your room to Johnny's club and from there to see Dulcy. So you must know about the knife."

He stopped talking and they waited for Chink to answer.

Chink didn't speak.

Suddenly, without warning, Coffin Ed stepped forward from the shadows and chopped Chink across the back of his neck with the edge of his hand. It knocked Chink forward, stunning him, and Coffin Ed grabbed him beneath the arms to keep him from falling on his face.

Grave Digger slid quickly from the desk and handcuffed Chink's ankles, drawing the bracelets tight just above the ankle bones. Then Coffin Ed handcuffed Chink's hands behind his back.

Without saying another word, they opened the door, lifted Chink from the chair and hung him upside down from the top of the door by his handcuffed ankles, so that the top part of the door split his legs down to his crotch. His back lay flat against the bottom edge, with the lock bolt sticking into him.

Then Grave Digger inserted his heel into Chink's left armpit and Coffin Ed did the same with his right, and they pushed down gradually.

126

Chink thought about the ten thousand dollars that Dulcy was going to get for him that day and tried to stand it. He tried to scream, but he had waited too late. All that came out was his tongue and he couldn't get it back. He began choking, and his eyes began to bulge.

"Let's take him down now," Grave Digger said.

They lifted him down and stood him on his feet, but he couldn't stand. He pitched forward. Grave Digger caught him before he hit the floor and lifted him back onto the stool.

"All right, spill it," Coffin Ed said. "And it'd better be straight."

Chink swallowed. "Okay," he said in a gasping voice. "I gave her the knife."

Coffin Ed's burnt face contorted with rage. Chink ducked automatically, but Coffin Ed merely clenched and opened his fists.

"When did you give it to her?" Grave Digger asked.

"It was just like the preacher said," Chink confessed. "One of the club members, Mr. Burns, brought it back from London and gave it to me for a Christmas present, and I gave it to her."

"What for?" Coffin Ed asked.

"Just for a gag," Chink said. "She's so scared of Johnny I thought it'd be a good joke."

"Damn right," Grave Digger said sourly. "It would have been awfully funny if you'd found it stuck between your own ribs."

"I didn't figure she'd let Johnny find it," Chink said.

"How do you know he found it?" Coffin Ed asked.

"We haven't got time for guesses," Grave Digger said.

They removed the handcuffs from Chink's wrists and ankles and booked him on suspicion of murder.

Then they tried to contact the Mr. Burns whom he said had given him the knife to verify the story. But the night clerk at the University Club said, in reply to their phone call, that Mr. Burns was in Europe somewhere.

They went back to Johnny's flat, rang the bell and hammered on the door. No one answered. They tried the service door. Grave Digger listened with his ear to the panel.

"Quiet as a grave," he said.

"Something's happened to the dog," Coffin Ed said.

They looked at one another.

"If we go in without a search warrant it's going to be risky," Grave Digger said. "If he's in there and he's already killed her, we're going to have to kill him. And if he hasn't done anything to her at all and they're both in there just keeping quiet and we break in, there's going to be hell to pay. He's liable to get us busted down to harness."

"I just hate to have Johnny kill his woman and go to the chair on account of a rat-tail punk like Chink," Coffin Ed said. "For all we know she might have killed Val herself. But if Johnny finds out she got the knife from Chink, her life ain't worth a damn."

"Chink might be lying," Grave Digger suggested.

"If he is, he'd better disappear from the face of the earth," Coffin Ed said.

"We'd better go in the front way then," Grave Digger said. "If Johnny's laying in there in the dark with his heater we'll have a better chance in that straight hall."

The door was framed on both sides and at the top by heavy iron angle-bars, making it impossible to pry open, and it was secured by three separate Yale locks.

It took Coffin Ed fifteen minutes working with seven master keys before he got it open.

They stood flanking the door with drawn revolvers while Grave Digger pushed it open with his foot. No sound came from the dark tunnel of the hall.

There was a chain-bolt on the door which, when fastened, kept it from opening more than a crack, but it hadn't been fastened.

"The chain's off," Grave Digger said. "He's not here."

"Don't take any chances," Coffin Ed warned.

"What the hell! Johnnys no lunatic," Grave Digger said, and walked into the dark hall. "It's me, Digger, and Ed Johnson, if you're in here, Johnny," he said quietly, felt for the light switch and turned on the hall light.

Their eyes went straight to a hasp and staple fitted to the outside of the master-bedroom door. It was fastened with a heavy brass Yale padlock. Coffin Ed closed the outside door, and they went down the hall and listened with their ears against the panel of the bedroom door. The only sound from within came from a radio tuned to an all-night disk jockey program of swing music.

"Anyway, she ain't dead," Grave Digger said. "He wouldn't lock up a corpse."

"But he's got hold of something or else he's blowing his top," Coffin Ed replied.

"Let's see what's in the rest of the house," Grave Digger suggested.

They started with the sitting room across the front and worked back to the kitchen. None of the rooms had been cleaned or straightened. The broken glass from the overturned cocktail table lay on the sitting-room carpet.

"Looks like it got kind of rough," Coffin Ed observed.

"It could be he's beaten her up," Grave Digger conceded.

The two bedrooms were across the hall from the kitchen and were separated by the bathroom. There, doors from each opened into the bathroom, which could be bolted from both sides. The door leading into the room Val had occupied was ajar, but the one to the master bedroom was bolted. Grave Digger slipped the bolt and they went in.

The shades were drawn and the room was dark save for a faint glow from the radio dial.

Coffin Ed switched on the light.

Dulcy lay on her side with her knees drawn up and her hands between her legs. She had kicked the covers off, and her nude sepia body had the dull sheen of metal. She was breathing silently, but her face was greasy from sweat and saliva had drooled from the bottom corner of her mouth.

"Sleeping like a baby," Grave Digger said.

"A drunken baby," Coffin Ed amended.

"Smells it, too," Grave Digger admitted.

There was an empty brandy bottle on the carpet beside the bed and an overturned glass in the center of a wet stain.

Coffin Ed crossed to the single window opening onto the inside fire escape and parted the drapes. The heavy iron grille on the outside of the window was padlocked.

He turned and came back to the bed. "Do you think this sleeping beauty knows she's been locked in?" he asked.

"Hard to say," Grave Digger admitted. "How do you figure it?"

"The way I figure it is Johnny's on to something, but he doesn't know what," Coffin Ed said. "He's out scouting about trying to find out something, and he's locked her up just in case he finds out the wrong thing."

"Do you think he knows about the knife?"

"If he does, he's out looking for Chink, and that's for sure," Coffin Ed said.

"Let's see what she's got to say," Grave Digger suggested, shaking her by the shoulder.

She awakened and brushed at her face drunkenly.

"Wake up, little sister," Grave Digger said.

"Go way," she muttered without opening her eyes. "Done give you all I got." Suddenly she giggled. "All but you-know-what. Ain't never going to give you none of that, nigger. That's all for Johnny."

Grave Digger and Coffin Ed looked at each other.

"I don't figure this at all," Grave Digger admitted.

"Maybe we'd better take her in," Coffin Ed ventured.

"We could, but if it turns out later that we're wrong and Johnny hasn't got anything against her other than just being normally jealous—"

"What do you call being normally jealous?" Coffin Ed interrupted. "You call locking up your woman being normally jealous?"

"For Johnny, anyway," Grave Digger said. "And if he comes back and finds we've broken into his house and arrested his woman—"

"On suspicion of murder," Coffin Ed interrupted again.

"Not even that would save us from a suspension. It's not as if we were picking her up off the street. We've broken into her house, and there's no evidence of a crime having been committed in here. And we'd need a warrant even if the charge were murder itself."

"Well, the only thing to do is to find him before he finds out what he's looking for," Coffin Ed acceded.

"Yeah, and we'd better get going because time is getting short," Grave Digger said.

They went back through the bathroom, leaving the door

wide open, and locked the front door with only the automatic lock.

First they went to the garage on 155th Street where Johnny kept his fishtail Cadillac, but he hadn't been in. Then they went by his club. It was dark and closed.

Next they began touring the cabarets, the dice games, the after-hours joints. They dropped the word they were looking for Chink Charlie.

The bartender at Small Paradise Inn said, "I ain't seen Chink all evening. He must be in jail. You looked for him there?"

"Hell, that's the last place cops ever look for anybody," Grave Digger said.

"Let's see if he's gone home yet," Coffin Ed suggested finally.

They went back to the flat, rang the bell. Receiving no answer they went in again. It was just as they had left it. Dulcy was sleeping in the same position. The radio station was signing off.

Coffin Ed looked at his watch. "It's four o'clock," he said. "Nothing for it now but to call it a day."

They drove back to the precinct station and made out their report. The lieutenant on charge at night sent for them and read the report before letting them off.

"Hadn't we better pick up the Perry woman?" he said.

"Not without a warrant," Grave Digger said. "We haven't been able to verify Chink Charlie Dawson's story about the knife, and if he's lying she can sue us for false arrest."

"What the hell," the lieutenant said. "You sound like she's Mrs. Vanderbilt."

"Maybe she's not Mrs. Vanderbilt, but Johnny Perry carries his weight in this town," Grave Digger said. "And that's out of our precinct, anyway."

"Okay, I'll have the 152nd Street precinct station put a couple of men in the building to arrest Johnny when he shows," the lieutenant said. "You fellows get some sleep. You've earned it."

"Anything yet from Chicago on Valentine Haines?" Grave Digger asked.

"Not a thing," the lieutenant said.

The sky was overcast when they left the station, and the air was hot and muggy.

"It looks like it's going to rain cats and dogs," Grave Digger said.

"Let it come down," Coffin Ed said.

18

MAMIE PULLEN WAS having breakfast when the telephone rang. She had a plate full of fried fish and boiled rice, and was dipping hot biscuits into a mixture of melted butter and blackstrap sorghum molasses.

Baby Sis had finished her breakfast an hour before, and was filling Mamie's cup from a pot of leftover coffee that had been boiling on the stove.

"Go answer it," Mamie said sharply. "Just don't stand there like a lump on a log."

"I just don't seem to be able to get myself together this mawning," Baby Sis said as she shuffled from the kitchen, through the sitting room, into the bedroom at the front.

When she returned Mamie was sipping jet-black coffee hot enough to scald a fowl.

"It's Johnny," she said.

Mamie was holding her breath as she got up from the table.

She was dressed in a faded red-flannel kimono and a pair of Big Joe's old working shoes. On her head she wore a black cotton stocking, knotted in the middle and hanging down her back.

"What you doing up so soon?" she asked into the phone. "Or has you gone to bed yet?"

"I'm in Chicago," Johnny said. "I flew here this morning."

Mamie's thin old body began trembling violently beneath the slack folds of the rusty old kimono, and the telephone shook in her hands as though she had the palsy.

"Trust her, son," she pleaded in a whining voice. "Trust her. She loves you."

"I trust her," Johnny said in his flat toneless voice. "How much trust am I supposed to have?"

"Then let it alone son," she begged. "You got her all for yourself. Ain't that enough?"

"I don't know whether I got her all for myself or not," he said. "That's what I want to find out."

"Ain't no good ever come from digging up the past," she warned.

"You tell me what it is and I'll stop digging," he said.

"Tell you what, son?"

"Whatever in the hell it is," he said. "If I knew I wouldn't be here."

"What is you want to know?"

"I just want to know what it is she thinks I'll pay ten grand for her to tell me," he said.

"You got it all wrong, Johnny," she argued in a moaning voice. "That's just Doll Baby lying to try to make herself look big. If Val was alive he'd tell you she was lying."

"Yeah. But he ain't alive," Johnny said. "And I got to find out for myself whether she's lying or not."

"But Val must have told you something," she said, sobbing deep in her thin old chest. "He must of told you something or else——" She broke off and began to swallow as though to swallow the words she'd already said.

"Or else what?" he asked in his toneless voice.

She kept swallowing until she could say finally, "Well, it's got to be something that you went all the way to Chicago for, 'cause it can't just be what a lying little bitch like Doll Baby says."

"All right then, what about you?" he said. "You ain't been lying. What you keep pleading Dulcy's case for then, if there ain't nothing to plead for?"

"I just don't want to see no more trouble, son," she moaned. "I just don't want to see no more blood spilt. Whatever it might have been, it's over with and she's all yours now, you can believe that."

"You ain't doing nothing but just adding to the mystery," he said.

133

"There ain't never been any mystery," she argued. "Not on her part. Not unless you made it."

"Okay, I made it," he said. "Let's drop it. What I called to tell you was I got her locked up in the bedroom—"

"Good Lord above!" she exclaimed. "What good you think that's going to do?"

"Just listen to me," he said. "The door's padlocked from the outside with a Yale lock. The key is on the kitchen shelf. I want you to go and let her out long enough to get something to eat and then lock her up again."

"Lord have mercy, son," she said. "How long do you think you can keep her locked up like that?"

"Until I straighten out some of these mysteries," he said. "That ought to be before the day's over."

"Don't forget one thing, son," she pleaded. "She loves you."

"Yeah," he said, and hung up.

Mamie dressed quickly in her black satin Mother Hubbard and her own men's shoes, dipped her bottom lip full of snuff and took the snuff stick and box of snuff along with her.

The sky was black-dark like an eclipse of the sun, and the street lights were still burning. Not a grain of dust nor a scrap of paper moved in the still close air. People walked about silently, in slow motion, like a city full of ghosts, and cats and dogs tiptoed from garbage can to garbage can as though afraid their footsteps might be heard. Before she found an empty taxi she felt herself suffocating from the exhaust fumes that didn't rise ten feet above the pavement.

"It's going to rain tadpoles and bull frogs," the colored driver said.

"It'll be a blessing," she said.

She had her own set of keys to the apartment, but it took her a long time to get in because Grave Digger and Coffin Ed had left the locks unlocked and she locked them thinking she was opening them.

When finally she got inside she had to sit for a moment in the kitchen to steady her trembling. Then she took the key from the shelf and unlocked the bedroom door from the hall. She noticed that the bathroom door was standing

134

open but her thoughts were so confused it held no meaning for her.

Dulcy was still asleep.

Mamie covered her with a sheet and took the empty brandy bottle and glass back to the kitchen. She began cleaning the house to occupy her mind.

It was ten minutes to twelve and she was scrubbing the kitchen floor when the thunderstorm broke. She drew the shades, put away the scrub brush and pail and sat at the table with her head bowed low and began to pray,

"Lord, show them the way, show them the light, don't let him kill nobody else."

The sound of the thunder had awakened Dulcy, and she stumbled toward the kitchen, calling in a frightened voice, "Spookie. Here, Spookie."

Mamie looked up from the table. "Spookie ain't here," she said.

Dulcy gave a start at sight of her. "Oh, it's you!" she exclaimed. "Where's Johnny?"

"Didn't he tell you?" Mamie asked.

"Tell me what?"

"He flew to Chicago."

Dulcy's eyes widened with terror and her face blanched to a muddy yellow. She flopped into a chair, but got up the next instant, got a bottle of brandy and a glass from the cabinet and gulped a stiff drink to quiet her trembling. But she kept on trembling. She brought the bottle and glass back to the table and sat down again and poured herself half a glass and started to drink it. Then she caught Mamie's look and put it down on the table. Her hand was trembling so violently the glass rattled on the enameled table top.

"Put on some clothes, child," Mamie said compassionately. "You're shaking from cold."

"I ain't cold," Dulcy denied. "I'm just scared to death, Aunt Mamie."

"I am, too, child," Mamie said. "But put on some clothes anyway, you ain't decent."

Dulcy got up without replying and went into the bedroom and put on a yellow flannel robe and matching mules. When she returned she picked up the glass and gulped the brandy down. She choked and sat down, gasping for breath.

Mamie dipped another lipful of snuff.

They sat silently without looking at each other.

Then Dulcy poured another drink.

"Don't, child," Mamie begged her. "Drinking ain't going to help none."

"Well, you got your lip full of snuff," Dulcy charged.

"That ain't the same thing," Mamie said. "Snuff purifies the blood."

"Alamena must have took her with her," Dulcy said. "Spookie, I mean."

"Didn't Johnny say nothing at all to you?" Mamie asked. A sudden clap of thunder made her shudder and she moaned, "God above, the world's coming to an end."

"I don't know what he said," Dulcy confessed. "All I know is he came sneaking in the back door and that's the last thing I remember."

"Was you alone?" Mamie asked fearfully.

"Alamena was here," Dulcy said. "She must have taken Spookie home with her." Then suddenly she caught Mamie's meaning. "My God, Aunt Mamie, you must think I'm a whore!" she exclaimed.

"I'm just trying to find out why he flew to Chicago all of a sudden," Mamie said.

"To check up on me," Dulcy said, gulping her drink defiantly. "For what else? He's always trying to check up on me. That's all he ever does, just check up on me." A roll of thunder rattled the windowpanes. "My God, I can't stand all that thunder!" she cried, jumping to her feet. "I got to go to bed."

She grabbed the brandy bottle and glass and fled to the bedroom. Lifting the top of the combination radio and record player, she put on a record, got into the bed and pulled the covers up to her eyes.

Mamie followed after a moment and sat in the chair beside the bed.

The wailing voice of Bessie Smith began to pour into the room over the sound of the rain beating against the windowpanes:

When it rain five days an' de skies turned dark as night

136

When it rain five days an' de skies turned dark as night
Then trouble taken place in the lowland that night

"Don't you even know why he locked you up?" Mamie asked.

Dulcy reach over and turned the player down.

"Now, what'd you say?" she asked.

"Johnny had you padlocked in this room," Mamie said. "He phoned me from Chicago to come over and let you out. That's how come I knew he was in Chicago."

"That ain't nothing strange for him," Dulcy said. "He's chained me to the bed."

Mamie began to sob quietly to herself. "Child, what's happening?" she asked. "What happened here last night to send him off like that?"

"Ain't nothing happened no more than usual," Dulcy said sullenly. Then after a moment she added, "You know that knife?"

"Knife? What knife?" Mamie looked blank.

"The knife what killed Val," Dulcy whispered.

Thunder rolled and Mamie gave a start. Rain slashed at the windows.

"Chink Charlie gave me a knife just like it," Dulcy said.

Mamie held her breath while Dulcy told her about the two knives, one of which Chink had given to her and the other he'd kept for himself. Then she sighed so profoundly with relief it sounded as though she were moaning again.

"Thank God then we know it was Chink who done it," she said.

"That's what I've been saying all along," Dulcy said. "But ain't nobody wanted to listen to me."

"But you can prove it, child," Mamie said. "All you got to do is show the police your knife and then they'll know it was his that killed him."

"But I ain't got mine no more," Dulcy said. "That's what I'm so scared of. I always kept it hidden in my lingerie drawer and then about two weeks ago it come up missing. And I been scared to ask anybody about it."

Mamie's complexion turned a strange ashy gray, and her face shrank until the skin was stretched tight against the bones. Her eyes looked sick and haggard.

"It just don't have to be Johnny what took it, does it?" she asked piteously.

"No, it don't have to be for sure," Dulcy said. "But there ain't nobody else who could have took it but Alamena. I don't know why she'd have taken it unless just to keep Johnny from finding it. Or else to have something to hold over me."

"You has a woman to come in here to clean," Mamie said.

"Yes, she could have taken it too," Dulcy admitted.

"It don't sound like Meeny," Mamie said. "So it must have been her. You tell me who she is, child, and if she took it I'll get it out of her."

They looked at one another through frightened, white-circled eyes.

"We just kidding ourselves, Aunt Mamie," Dulcy said. "Ain't nobody took that knife but Johnny."

Mamie looked at her and the tears rolled down her old ashy-black cheeks.

"Child, did Johnny know any reason to kill Val?" she asked.

"What reason could he have had?" Dulcy countered.

"I didn't ask what reason he could have had," Mamie said. "I asked what reason he might have known about."

Dulcy slid down into the bed until only her eyes were showing above the covers, but still she couldn't meet Mamie's gaze. She looked away.

"He didn't know of none," she said. "He liked Val."

"Tell me truth, child," Mamie insisted.

"If he did," Dulcy whispered. "He didn't learn it from me."

The record played out and Dulcy started it over again.

"Did you ask Johnny to give you ten thousand dollars to get rid of Val?" Mamie asked.

"Jesus Christ no!" Dulcy flared. "That whore's just lying about that!"

"You're not holding anything back on me, are you, child?" Mamie asked.

"I might ask you the same thing," Dulcy said.

"About what, child?"

138

"How could Johnny have found out, if he did find out, if you didn't tell him?"

"I didn't tell him," Mamie said. "And I know Big Joe didn't tell him because he'd just found out himself and he up and died before he had a chance to tell anybody."

"Somebody must have told him," Dulcy said.

"Then maybe it was Chink," Mamie said.

"It wasn't Chink 'cause he don't know," Dulcy said. "All Chink knows about is the knife and he's trying to blackmail me for ten grand. He claims if I don't get it for him he's going to tell Johnny." Dulcy began laughing hysterically. "As if that'd make any difference if Johnny knows about the other."

"Stop that laughing," Mamie said sharply and reached over and slapped her.

"Johnny will kill him," she added.

"I wish Johnny would," Dulcy said viciously. "If he don't really know about the other then that would settle everything."

"There must be some other way," Mamie said. "If the Lord will just show us the light. You can't just settle everything by killing people."

"If he just doesn't already know," Dulcy said.

The recording played out and she put it on again.

"For God's sake, child, can't you play something else," Mamie said. "That tune gives me the willies."

"I like it," Dulcy said. "It's just as blue as I feel."

They listened to the wailing voice and the intermittent sound of thunder from without.

The afternoon wore on. Dulcy kept on drinking, and the level of the bottle went down and down. Mamie dipped snuff. Every now and then one of them would speak and the other would answer listlessly.

No one telephoned. No one called.

Dulcy played the one recording over and over and over. Bessie Smith sang:

> *Backwater blues done cause me to pack mah things*
> *an' go*
> *Backwater blues done cause me to pack mah things*
> *an' go*

"Jesus Christ, I wish he'd come on home and kill me and get it over with if that's what he wants to do!" Dulcy cried.

The front door was unlocked and Johnny came into the flat. He walked into the bedroom wearing the same green silk suit and rose crepe shirt he'd worn to the club the night before, but now it was wrinkled and soiled. His .38 caliber automatic pistol made a lump in his right coat-pocket. His hands were empty. His eyes burned like live coals but looked tired, and the veins stood out like roots from his graying temples. The scar on his forehead was swollen but still. He needed a shave, and the gray hairs in his beard glistened whitely against his dark skin. His face was expressionless.

He grunted as his eyes took in the scene, but he didn't speak. The two women watched him with fear-stricken eyes, unmoving, as he crossed the room and turned off the record player, then parted the drapes and raised the window. The storm had stopped, and the afternoon sun was reflected from the windows across the airwell.

Finally he came around the bed, kissed Mamie on the forehead and said, "Thanks, Aunt Mamie, you can go home now." His voice was expressionless.

Mamie didn't move. Her old, bluish-tinted eyes remained terror-stricken as they searched his face, but it revealed nothing.

"No," she said. "Let's talk it over now, while I'm here."

"Talk what over?" he said.

She stared at him.

Dulcy said defiantly, "Ain't you going to kiss me?"

Johnny looked at her as though studying her under a microscope. "Let's wait until you get sober," he said in his toneless voice.

"Don't do nothing, Johnny, I beg you on bending knees," Mamie said.

"Do what?" Johnny said, without taking his gaze from Dulcy.

"For God's sake, don't look at me as though I crucified Christ," Dulcy whimpered. "Go ahead and do whatever you want to do, just quit looking at me."

140

"I don't want you to say I took advantage of you while you were drunk," he said. "Let's wait until you get sober."

"Son, listen to me—" Mamie began, but Johnny cut her off. "All I want to do is sleep," he said. "How long do you think I can go without sleeping?"

He took the pistol from his pocket, put it beneath his pillow and began stripping off his clothes before Mamie had got up from the chair.

"Leave these in the kitchen as you go out," he said, giving her the near-empty brandy bottle and glass.

She took them away without further comment. He piled his clothes on the chair she'd vacated. His heavy brown muscles were tattoed with scars. When he'd stripped naked he set the radio alarm for ten o'clock, rolled Dulcy over and got into bed beside her. She tried to caress him but he pushed her away.

"There's ten G's in C-notes in my inside coat pocket," he said. "If that's what you want, just don't be here when I wake up."

He was asleep before Mamie left the house.

19

WHEN CHINK ENTERED the flat where he roomed, the telephone was ringing. He was grimy with dirt, unshaven, and his beige summer suit showed that he'd slept in it. His yellow skin looked like a greasy paste lined with wrinkles where the witches had ridden him in his sleep. There were big black half moons beneath his beaten muddy eyes.

His lawyer had taken all the money he'd gotten from Dulcy to get him out on bail again. He felt like a whipped cur, chagrined, deflated and humiliated. Now that he was out, he wasn't sure whether it wouldn't have been better for him to have stayed in jail. If the cops hadn't picked up Johnny he'd have to keep on the run, but no matter how much he ran there was no place in Harlem where he could hide. Everybody would be against him when they found out he'd turned rat.

"It's for you, Chink," the landlady called to him.

He went into the bedroom where she kept her telephone, with a padlock on the dial.

"Hello," he said in a mean voice and gave his landlady a mean look for lingering in the room.

She went out and closed the door.

"It's me, Dulcy," the voice from the telephone said.

"Oh!" he said and his hands began to shake.

"I've got the money," she said.

"What!" He looked as though someone had stuck a gun in his belly and asked him if he wanted to bet it wasn't loaded. "Ain't he been arrested?" he asked involuntarily before he could catch himself.

"Arrested?" Her voice sounded suddenly suspicious. "Why the hell should he be arrested? Unless you've ratted about the knife."

"You know damn well I ain't ratted," he declared. "You think I'm going to blow away ten grand?" Thinking fast, he added, "It's just I ain't seen him around all day."

"He's gone to Chicago to check up on me and Val," she said.

"Then how'd you get the ten grand?" he wanted to know.

"That's none of your business," she said.

He suspected a trap, but the thought of getting ten thousand dollars filled him with a reckless greed. He had to hold himself in. He felt as though he were going to explode with exultation. All his life he'd wanted to be a big shot, and now was his chance if he played his cards right.

"Okay," he said. "I don't give a damn how you got it, whether you stole it or cut his throat for it, just so long as you've got it."

"I've got it," she said. "But you'll have to bring me your knife before I'll give it to you."

"What the hell do you think I am?" he said. "You bring me the money here and we'll talk about the knife."

"No, you've got to come here to the house and get the money and bring me the knife," she said.

"I ain't that crazy, baby," he said. "It ain't that I'm scared of Johnny, but I don't have to take no rape-fiend chance like that. It's your little tail that's in the vise, and you're goin' to have to pay to get it out."

"Listen, honey, there ain't no chance in it," she said. "He can't get back before tomorrow night because it's going to take him all day tomorrow to find out what he's looking for, and when he gets back I got to be gone myself."

"I don't dig you," Chink said.

"You ain't so smart then, honey," she said. "What he's going to find out is what caused Val to wind up dead."

Suddenly Chink began to see the light. "Then it was you—"

She cut him off. "What difference does it make now? I got to be gone when he gets back, and that's for sure. I just want to leave him a souvenir."

An expression of triumph lit Chink's face. "You mean you want me, there in his own house?"

"In his own bed," she said. "The mother-raper always suspected me of cheating on him when I wasn't. Now I'm going to fix him."

Chink gave a low vicious laugh. "You and me, baby, we're going to fix him together."

"Well, hurry up then," she said.

"Give me half an hour," he said.

She had unhooked the extension in the bedroom and was talking from the extension in the kitchen. When she hung up she said to herself, "You asked for it."

Dulcy was watching from the peephole and opened the door before he rang. She wore her robe with nothing underneath.

"Come on in, honey," she said. "The place is ours."

"I knew I'd get you," he said, making a grab at her, but she slipped neatly out of his arms and said, "All right then, don't make me wait."

He looked into the kitchen.

"If you're scared, search the house," she said.

"Who's scared?" he said belligerently.

The bedroom which Val had used was directly across from the kitchen and the master bedroom beyond the bathroom, adjoining the sitting room.

She started to lead Chink into Val's room, but he went up to the front and looked into the sitting room, then he hesitated before the door to the master bedroom. Dulcy had padlocked it with the heavy Yale lock Johnny had used to lock her in.

"What's in there?" Chink asked.

"That was Val's room," Dulcy said.

"What's it doing locked?" he wanted to know.

"The police locked it," she said. "If you want it open, go ahead and break down the door."

He laughed, then looked into the bathroom. The water was running in the tub.

"I'm going to take a bath first," she said. "Do you mind?"

He kept on laughing to himself with a crazy sort of exultation.

"You're a real bitch," he said, taking her by the arms and pushing her into Val's bedroom and back across the bed. "I knew you were a bitch, but I didn't know how much bitch you really are."

He began kissing her.

"Let me take a bath first," she said. "I stink."

He laughed jubilantly, as though laughing to himself at his own private joke.

"A real solid-gold bitch," he said as though talking to himself. Then suddenly he sat up straight. "Where's the money?"

"Where's the knife?" she countered.

He took it from his pocket and held it in his hand.

She pointed to an envelope on the dressing table.

He picked it up, opened it with one hand while holding onto the knife with the other and shook hundred dollar bills onto the bedspread. She eased the knife from his hand and slipped it into the pocket of her robe, but he didn't notice. He was rooting his face in the money like a hog in swill.

144

"Put it away and undress," she said.

He stood up, laughing crazily to himself, and began stripping off his clothes.

"I'll just leave it there and look at it," he said.

She sat at the dressing table and massaged her face with cream until he'd finished undressing.

But instead of getting beneath the covers he lay on top of the coverlet, and he kept picking up the brand-new money and letting it rain down over his naked body like falling leaves.

"Have a good time," she said, going into the bathroom. She heard him laughing crazily to himself as she closed the adjoining door.

She quickly stepped across the bathroom, opened the opposite door and stepped into the other bedroom.

Johnny slept on his back with one arm flung out across the cover and the other folded loosely across his stomach. He snored lightly.

She closed the bathroom door behind her, crossed the room quietly, and set the radio to alarm within five minutes. Then she dressed quickly in a slack suit without stopping to put on underwear, slipped into the robe again, and went back into the bathroom.

The water had been running all the while and had reached the overflow outlet. She turned off the faucet, turned on the shower and pulled the drain stopper.

Then she went quickly into the hall, turned into the kitchen, took her saddle-leather shoulder handbag from one of the cabinet shelves and went out through the service doorway.

She was crying so hard as she ran down the stairs she bumped into two uniformed white cops coming up. They stood aside to let her pass.

145

20

THE RADIO CAME on with a blast.

Some big brassy band was beating out a rock and roll rhythm.

Johnny came awake as though he'd been bitten by a snake, leaped out of the bed and grabbed for the pistol underneath his pillow.

Then he realized it was only the radio. He grunted sheepishly and noticed that Dulcy was out of bed. He felt his inside coat pocket with his free hand, still holding the pistol in his right hand, and discovered the ten thousand dollars were gone.

He patted the coat absently where it lay on the chair beside the bed, but he was looking at the empty bed. His breath came shallowly, but his face was expressionless.

"Sevened out," he said to himself. "You lost that bet."

The radio was playing so loudly he didn't hear the door to the bathroom open. He merely caught a flicker of movement from the corner of his eye and turned.

Chink stood naked, with his eyes dilated and his mouth wide open, in the doorway.

They stared at each other until the moment ran out.

Suddenly the veins popped out in Johnny's temples as though they were about to explode. The scar ballooned out from his forehead and the tentacles wriggled as though trying to free themselves from his head. Then a blinding flash went off inside of his skull as though his brains had been dynamited.

His brain made no record of his next actions.

He squeezed the trigger of his .38 automatic until it had pumped all its slugs into Chink's stomach, lungs, heart and head. Then he leaped across the floor and stomped Chink's dying bloody body with his bare feet until two of Chink's teeth were stuck into his calloused heel. After that he leaned over and clubbed Chink's head into a bloody pulp with his pistol butt.

But he didn't know he had done it.

The next thing he knew consciously after having first caught sight of Chink was that he was being held forcibly by two white uniformed cops and Chink's bloody corpse lay on the floor in the doorway, half in the bedroom and half in the bathroom, and the shower was pouring down into an empty tub.

"Turn me loose so I can dress," he said in his toneless voice. "You can't take me to jail buck naked."

The cops freed him and he began to dress.

"We've called precinct and they're sending over some jokers from Homicide," one of them said. "You want to buzz your mouthpiece before they get here?"

"What for?" Johnny said, without stopping dressing.

"We heard the shots and the back door was open, so we came on in," the other cop said half apologetically. We thought maybe it was her you'd shot."

Johnny said nothing. He was dressed before the men from Homicide arrived.

They held him there until Detective Sergeant Brody came.

"Well, you killed him," Brody said.

"There's all the evidence," Johnny said.

They took him back to the 116th Street Precinct station for questioning because Grave Digger and Coffin Ed were on the case and they worked out of that station.

Brody sat as before behind the desk in the Pigeon Nest. Grave Digger was perched on the edge of the desk, and Coffin Ed stood in the shadow in the corner.

It was 8:37 o'clock and still light outside, but it didn't make any difference to them because the room didn't have any windows.

Johnny sat in the spill of light on the stool in the center of the room, facing Brody. The vertical light made grotesque patterns of the scar on his forehead and the veins swelling from his temples, but his big muscular body

147

was relaxed and his face was expressionless. He looked like a man who'd gotten a load from his shoulders.

"Why don't you just let me tell you what I know," he said in his toneless voice. "If you don't buy it, you can question me afterwards."

"Okay, shoot," Brody said.

"Let's begin with the knife, and get that cleared up with," Johnny said. "I found the knife in her drawer on a Tuesday afternoon a little over two weeks ago. I just thought she'd bought it to protect herself from me. I put it in my pocket and took it to the club. Then I got to thinking about it and I was going to put it back, but Big Joe seen it. If she was so scared of me she needed to keep a skinner's knife hidden in the drawer where she kept her underwear, I was going to let her keep it. But I was handling it and Big Joe said he'd like to have a knife like that, and I gave it to him. That's the last I seen it or even thought about it until you showed it to me here on that desk and said it was the knife that killed Val, and that the preacher had said he'd seen Chink when he gave it to her."

"You don't know what Big Joe did with it?" Brody asked.

"No, he never said. All he ever said was that if he carried it around he was scared he might get mad some day and cut somebody with it, and it was the kind of knife that would cut a man's head off when all you were trying to do was mark him."

"Did you ever see another knife like it?" Brody asked.

"Not exactly like it," Johnny said. "I've seen knives what look kind of like it, but none what look exactly like it."

Brody took the knife from the desk drawer as he had done the first time and pushed it across the desk.

"Is this the knife?"

Johnny leaned forward and picked it up.

"Yeah, but how it got stuck into Val, I couldn't say."

"This one wasn't stuck into Val," Brody said. "This one was found on a shelf in your kitchen cabinet less than a half hour ago." He then put the duplicate knife on the desk top. "This was the one found stuck in Val."

Johnny looked from one knife to the other without speaking.

"How do you account for that?" Brody asked.

"I don't know," Johnny said, without expression.

"Could Big Joe have left it in the house at some time, and somebody have put it on the shelf?" Brody asked.

"If he did, I don't know about it," Johnny said.

"All right, that's your story," Brody said. "Let's get back to Val. When was the last time you saw him?"

"It was about ten minutes of four when I came down from the club," Johnny said. "I'd been winning and the players didn't want me to quit, so I was late. Val was setting in the car waiting for me."

"Wasn't that unusual?" Brody interrupted.

Johnny looked at him.

"Why didn't he come up to the club?" Brody asked.

"Wasn't nothing strange 'bout that," Johnny said. "He liked to set in my car and play the radio. He had a set of keys, him and her both, just for emergency 'cause I never let him drive. And he's set in it by the hour. I suppose it made him feel like a big shot. I don't know how long he'd been setting there. I didn't ask him. He'd said he'd come from talking to Reverend Short and he had something to tell me. But we were late and I was afraid the wake would break up before we got there—"

"He said he'd been talking with Reverend Short?" Brody interrupted again. "At that time of night—morning, rather?"

"Yeah, but I didn't think anything about it at the time," Johnny replied. "I told him to stow it and tell me later, but just before we got to Seventh Avenue he said he didn't feel like going to the wake. He said he was going away, he was going to catch an early train to Chicago and he didn't know where he was going from there and I'd better listen to what he had to say 'cause it was important. I pulled up to the corner and parked. He said he'd been up to the preacher's church—if you call it a church; he'd met him there 'bout two o'clock that morning and they'd had a long talk. But before he'd got to say any more I saw a stud slipping along beside the parked cars across the street and I knew he was going to try to steal the A and P store manager's change poke. I said, wait a minute, let's watch this little play. There was a colored cop named Harris standing beside the manager while he unlocked the door, and there was some stud leaning out Big Joe's bedroom window watching the play, too. This stud lifted the poke from the car seat and took off, but the manager saw him, and he and the cop took off after him—"

Brody cut him off. "We know about that. What happened after Reverend Short got up?"

"I didn't know it was the preacher until he got up out of that breadbasket," Johnny said. "Funniest thing you ever saw. He got up and began shaking himself like a cat what's fell in a pile of dung. When I made out who he was I figured he was full of that wild cherry brandy and opium juice he drinks, then he took another drink from his bottle and went back into the house, tiptoeing and shaking himself like a wet-footed cat. Val was laughing, too. He said you can't hurt a drunk. Then all of a sudden I thought of how we could pull a good gag. I told Val to go across the street and lie down in the breadbasket where the preacher had fallen and I'd go around to Hamfat's all night joint and telephone Mamie and tell here there was a dead man there who'd fallen out of her window. Hamfat's place is on 135th and Lenox, and it wouldn't have taken me longer than five minutes to make the call. But some chick was using the phone and I figured by the time I got the call through somebody would have already found Val and the gag would have been lost—"

"How did you go to Hamfat's?" Brody interrupted.

"I drove," Johnny said. "I turned up Seventh Avenue to 135th Street and crossed over. I didn't know he'd been stabbed until Mamie told me on the phone."

"Did you see anyone coming from the house, or anyone at all on the street when you drove up Seventh Avenue?" Brody asked.

"Not a soul."

"Did you tell Mamie who you were?"

"No, I tried to disguise my voice. I knew she'd know it was a gag if she recognized my voice."

150

"You don't think she recognized it?" Brody insisted.

"I don't think so," Johnny said. "But I couldn't say."

"Okay, that's your story," Brody said. "Now what did you go to Chicago for?"

"I was trying to find out what it was Val wanted to tell me before he got himself killed," Johnny admitted. "After Doll Baby came to my house that afternoon right after the funeral and claimed that Val was going to get ten grand from me to open up a liquor store, I wanted to know what it was I was going to give him ten grand for to know. He never had a chance to tell me, and I had to find out for myself."

"Did you find out?" Brody asked, leaning forward slightly.

Grave Digger bent over from the waist as though to hear better, and Coffin Ed stepped forward from the shadows.

"Yeah," Johnny said in his toneless voice, his face remaining without expression. "He was her husband. I figure he was going to ask me for ten grand so he could go away. I figure he was going to take Doll Baby with him."

The three detectives remained alert, as though listening for a sound that would presage the instant of danger.

"Would you have given it to him?" Brody asked.

"Not so you could notice," Johnny said.

"Was it his idea or hers?" Brody insisted.

"I couldn't say," Johnny said. "I ain't God."

"Would she have done it for him if he had made her, tried to make her?" Brody kept on.

"I couldn't say," Johnny said.

Brody kept hammering. "Or would she have killed him?"

"I couldn't say," Johnny said in his toneless voice.

"What was Chink Charlie doing in your house?" Brody continued. "Was he blackmailing her about the knife?"

"I couldn't say," Johnny said.

"Ten thousand dollars in hundred-dollar bills were strewn over the bed in the other bedroom," Brody said. "Did he come to collect that?"

"I couldn't say what he come for," Johnny said. "You know what he got."

"It was your money," Brody persisted.

"No, it was hers," Johnny said. "I got it for her when I came back from Chicago. If all she wanted out of me was ten grand she was welcome to it. All she had to do was take it and get out. It was easier for me to go in debt to give her ten grand than to have to kill her."

"Do you have any idea where she might have gone?" Brody asked.

"I couldn't say," Johnny said. "She's got her own car, a Chevy convertible I gave her for Christmas. She could have gone anywhere."

"Okay, Johnny, that's all for now," Brody said. "We're going to hold you on manslaughter and suspicion of murder. You can telephone your lawyer now. Maybe he can get you out on bail."

"What for?" Johnny said. "All I want to do is sleep."

"You can sleep better at home," Brody said. "Or else go to a hotel."

"I sleep fine in jail," Johnny said. "It ain't like as if it was the first time."

When the jailors had taken Johnny away, Brody said, "It looks to me as if she's our little pet. She killed her legal husband to keep from fouling up her little gravy train. Then she had to set a trap and get her illegal husband to kill Chink Charlie, trying to save herself from the electric chair."

"What about the knife?" Coffin Ed said.

"She either had both knives, or else she got this one from Chink and left it there when she went out," Brody said.

"But why did she leave it there where it was sure to be found?" Coffin Ed persisted. "If she really had the second knife, why didn't she get rid of it? Then Johnny would be tapped for killing Val, too. He'd have to prove that he gave the knife to Big Joe, and Big Joe is dead. It would be an open and shut case against Johnny if it wasn't for the second knife."

"Maybe Johnny got the second knife and put it there

152

himself," Grave Digger said. "He's the smartest one of all."

"We should have done like I said and brought her in last night," Coffin Ed said.

"Let's quit guessing and second-guessing and go get her now," Grave Digger said.

"Right," Brody said. "In the meantime I'll go over all the reports."

"Don't take any unnecessary chances with those bad words," Coffin Ed said with a straight face.

"Yeah," Grave Digger amended with equal solemnity. "Don't let none of them sneak up behind you and stab you while you're not looking."

"What the hell!" Brody said, reddening. "You guys'll be out chasing the hottest piece of tail in Harlem. I envy you."

21

THEY FOUND MAMIE ironing the clothes Baby Sis had washed that morning. It was steaming in the kitchen from the pair of flatirons Mamie heated on her electric stove.

They told her Dulcy had left home, Johnny had killed Chink and was in jail.

She sat down and started moaning.

"Lord, I knowed there was goin' to be another killing," she said.

"Where would she go, now that both Chink and Val are dead and Johnny's locked up?" Grave Digger asked.

"Only the Lord knows," she said in a wailing voice. "She might have gone to see the reverend."

"Reverend Short!" Grave Digger said in a startled voice. "Why would she go to him?"

Mamie looked up in surprise. "Why, she's in deep trouble and he's a man of God. Dulcy's religious underneath. She might have gone to seek God in her misery."

Baby Sis giggled. Mamie gave her a threatening look.

"He is a man of God," Mamie said. "Only thing he drinks too much of that poison and sometimes it makes him a little crazy."

"If she's there, let's just hope he ain't too crazy," Coffin Ed said.

Five minutes later they were tiptoeing through the semidark of the store-front church. The shotgun hole in the door to Reverend Short's room at the rear had been closed by a piece of cardboard, shielding the light from within, but the croaking sound of Reverend Short's voice could be distinctly heard. They crept forward silently and bent toward the door to listen.

"But, Jesus Christ, why did you have to kill him?" they heard a blurred feminine voice exclaim.

"You are a harlot," they heard Reverend Short croak in reply. "I must save thy soul from hell. You are mine. I have slain thy husband. Now I must give you unto God."

"Crazy as a loon," Grave Digger said aloud.

There was a sound of sudden scurrying inside the room. "Who's there?" Reverend Short croaked in a voice as thin and dry as a rattlesnake's warning.

"The law," Grave Digger said, flattening himself against the wall beside the door. "Detectives Jones and Johnson. Come out with your hands up."

Before he'd finished speaking Coffin Ed was sprinting down the corridor between the benches to go outside and circle to the rear windows.

"You can't have her," Reverend Short croaked. "She belongs to God now."

"We don't want her. We want you," Grave Digger said.

"I'm God's instrument," Reverend Short said.

"I don't doubt that," Grave Digger said, trying to hold his attention until Coffin Ed had time to approach the rear windows. "All we want to do is see that you get back safe and sound into God's instrument case."

The shotgun blasted from inside, without the warning sound of being cocked, and blew a hole through the center of the door.

"You didn't get me," Grave Digger called. "Try the other barrel."

There was a sound of movement inside the room, and Dulcy screamed. The sound of two shots from a .38 revolver coming from the courtyard in back followed instantly. Grave Digger turned on the balls of his big flat feet, hit the door with his left shoulder and rocketed into the room with his long barreled nickel-plated .38 cocked and ready in his right hand. Reverend Short was sprawled face downward across the seat of the wooden chair beside the bed, trying to reach the shotgun, which lay on the floor half underneath the table. He was reaching for it with his left hand. His right hand dangled uselessly at his side.

Grave Digger leaned forward and hit him across the back of the head with his pistol barrel, just hard enough to knock him unconscious without braining him, then turned to give his attention to Dulcy before Reverend Short had rolled over and fallen to the floor.

She lay spread-eagled on the bed, her hands and feet tied to the bedposts with clothesline. Her torso and feet were bare, but she still wore the pants of a bright red slack suit. The bone handle of a knife was sticking straight up from the crevice between her breasts. She looked at Grave Digger from huge black terror-stricken eyes.

"I bad hurt?" she asked in a whisper.

"I doubt it," Grave Digger said, then looked at her closer and added, "You're too pretty to be bad hurt. Only ugly women ever get hurt bad."

Coffin Ed was tearing off the chicken-wire screen from the rear window. Grave Digger crossed the room and raised the window and finished kicking it out. Coffin Ed climbed inside.

Grave Digger said, "Let's get these beauties to the hospital."

Reverend Short was taken to the psychiatric ward of Bellevue Hospital downtown on First Avenue and 29th Street. He was given a shot of paraldehyde and was docile and rational when the detectives went in to wind up the case. He sat propped up in bed with his right arm in a sling.

Detective Sergeant Brody from Homicide had ridden downtown with Grave Digger and Coffin Ed, and he sat

155

beside the bed and did the questioning. The police reporter sat beside him.

Coffin Ed sat on the other side of the bed and stared down at the chart hanging at the foot. Grave Digger sat on the window sill and watched the tugboats chugging up and down the East River.

"Just a few little questions, Reverend," Brody said cheerfully. "First, why did you kill him?"

"God directed me to," Reverend Short replied in a calm, quiet voice.

Brody glanced at Coffin Ed, but Coffin Ed didn't notice. Grave Digger continued to stare out at the river.

"Tell us about it," Brody said.

"Big Joe Pullen found out that he was her husband and they were still living in sin while she was supposed to be married to Johnny Perry," Reverend Short began.

"When did he find that out?" Brody asked.

"On his last trip," Reverend Short said quietly. "He was going to talk to Val and tell him to clear out, go to Chicago, get his divorce quietly and just disappear. But before Joe Pullen had a chance to talk to him he died. When I came to help Mamie arrange for the funeral she told me what Big Joe had found out, and asked me for spiritual advice. I told her to leave it to me and I'd take care of it, being as I was both her and Big Joe's spiritual advisor and Johnny and Dulcy Perry were members of my church, too, although they never attended the services. I telephoned Val and told him I wanted to talk to him, and he said he didn't have time to talk to preachers. So I had to tell him what I wanted to talk to him about. He said he'd come and see me in my church the night of the wake, and we made an appointment for two o'clock. I think he was preparing to do me injury, but I was prepared, and I put it to him straight. I told him I'd give him twenty-four hours to get out of town and leave her alone or I'd tell Johnny. He told me he'd go. I was satisfied he was telling me the truth, so I went back to the wake to comfort Mamie in her last hours with Big Joe's mortal remains. It was while I was there that God directed me to slay him."

"How did that happen, Reverend?" Brody asked gently.

Reverend Short took off his glasses, laid them aside and

156

ran his hand down over his thin bony face. He put his glasses back on.

"I am give to receiving instructions from God, and I don't question them," he said. "While I was standing in the room where Big Joe's mortal remains lay in the casket, I felt an overwhelming urge to go into the front bedroom. I knew right away that God was sending me on some mission. I obeyed without reservation. I went into the bedroom and closed the door. Then I felt the urge to look among Big Joe's things . . ."

Coffin Ed slowly turned his head to stare at him. Grave Digger turned his gaze from the East River and stared at him, too. The police reporter glanced up quickly and down again.

"As I was looking through his things I came across the knife laying in his dresser drawer among his hairbrushes and safety razors and things. God told me to take it. I took it. I put it into my pocket. God told me to go to the window and look out. I went to the window and looked out. Then God caused me to fall—"

"As I remember it, you said before that Chink Charlie pushed you," Brody interrupted.

"That was what I thought then," Reverend Short said in his quiet voice. "But since then I've come to realize it was God who pushed me. I had the urge to fall, but I was holding back, and God had to give me a little push. Then God placed that basket of bread on the sidewalk to break my fall."

"Before you said it was the Body of Christ," Brody reminded him.

"Yes," Reverend Short admitted. "But since then I've communed with God and now I know it was bread. When I got out of the bread basket and found myself unhurt, I knew right away that God had placed me in that position to accomplish some task, but I didn't know what. So I stood in the hallway downstairs, out of sight, waiting for God to direct me what to do—"

"You're sure it wasn't just to take a leak," Coffin Ed cut in.

"Well, I did that, too," Reverend Short admitted. "I have a weak bladder."

"No wonder," Grave Digger said.

"Let him go on," Brody said.

"While I was waiting for God to instruct me, I saw Valentine Haines crossing the street," Reverend Short said. "I knew right away that God wanted me to do something about him. I stood out of sight and watched him from the shadows. Then I saw him walk up to the bread basket and lie down as though to go to sleep. He lay just as though he were lying in a coffin awaiting his burial. I knew then what it was that God wanted me to do. I opened the knife and held it up my sleeve and stepped outside. Val saw me right away and said, I thought you went back upstairs to the wake, Reverend. I said, no, I've been waiting for you. He said, waiting for me for what. I said, waiting to kill you in the name of the Lord, and I leaned down and stabbed him in the heart."

Sergeant Brody exchanged glances with the two colored detectives.

"Well, that wraps it up," he said, then, turning back to Reverend Short, he remarked cynically, "I suppose you'll cop a plea of insanity."

"I'm not insane," Reverend Short said serenely. "I'm holy."

"Yeah," Brody said. He turned to the police reporter. "Get a copy of that statement typed for him to sign as soon as possible."

"Right," the police reporter said, closing his notebook and hurrying from the room.

Brody rang for the attendant and left him with Grave Digger and Coffin Ed. Outside he turned to Grave Digger and said, "You were right after all when you said that folks in Harlem do things for reasons nobody else in the world would think of."

Grave Digger grunted.

"Do you think he's really crazy?" Brody persisted.

"Who knows?" Grave Digger said.

"Depends on what you mean by crazy," Coffin Ed amended.

"He was just sexually frustrated and lusting after a married woman," Grave Digger said. "When you get to mixing sex and religion it will make anybody crazy."

"If he sticks to his story, he'll beat it," Brody said.

"Yeah," Coffin Ed said bitterly. "And if the cards had fallen just a little differently Johnny Perry would have got burned."

Dulcy had been taken to Harlem hospital. Her wound was superficial. The knife thrust had been stopped by her sternum.

But they kept her in the hospital because she could pay for a room.

She telephoned Mamie and Mamie went to her immediately. She cried her heart out on Mamie's shoulder, while telling her the story.

"But why didn't you just get rid of Val, child?" Mamie asked her. "Why didn't you send him away."

"I wasn't sleeping with him," Dulcy said.

"It didn't make any difference—he was still your husband and you kept him there in the house."

"I felt sorry for him, that's all," Dulcy said. "He wasn't worth a damn for nothing, but I felt sorry for him just the same."

"Well, for God's sake, child," Mamie said. "Anyway, why didn't you tell the police about Chink having another knife instead of getting Johnny to kill him?"

"I know I should have done it," Dulcy confessed. "But I didn't know what to do."

"Then why didn't you go to Johnny, child, and make a clean breast and ask him what to do?" Mamie said. "He was your man, child. He was the only one for you to go to."

"Go to Johnny!" Dulcy said, laughing with an edge of hysteria. "Imagine me going to Johnny with that story. I thought he had done it himself."

"He would have listened to you," Mamie said. "You ought to know Johnny that well by now, child."

"It wasn't that, Aunt Mamie," Dulcy sobbed. "I know he would have listened. But he would have hated me."

"There, there, don't cry," Mamie said, caressing her hair. "It's all over now."

"That's what I mean," Dulcy said. "It's all over." She buried her face in her hands and sobbed heartbrokenly.

"I love the ugly bastard," she said sobbingly. "But I ain't got no way to prove it."

It was a hot morning. The neighborhood kids were playing in the street.

Johnny's lawyer, Ben Williams, had got him out on bail. The garage had sent a man down to the jail with his fishtail Cadillac. Johnny came out and got in behind the wheel and the man from the garage sat in back. The lawyer sat beside Johnny.

"We'll get that manslaughter charge nol-prossed," the lawyer said. "You ain't got a thing to worry about."

Johnny pressed the starter, shifted to drive, and the big convertible moved off slowly.

"That ain't what I'm worrying about," he said.

"What is it?" the lawyer asked.

"You wouldn't know anything about it," Johnny said.

Skinny black kids in their summer shifts ran after the big flashy Cadillac, touching it with love and awe.

"Fishtail Johnny Perry," they called after him. "Four Ace Johnny Perry."

He threw up his left hand in a sort of salute.

"Try me," the lawyer said. "I'm supposed to be your brain."

"How can a jealous man win?" Johnny said.

"By trusting his luck," the lawyer said. "You're the one who's the gambler, you ought to know that."

"Well, pal," Johnny said. "You'd better be right."

Printed in the United States
by Baker & Taylor Publisher Services